WAR 4: SKULL ISLAND                    1

WAR

FOUR
SKULL ISLAND

NATIONAL BESTSELLING AUTHOR

T. STYLES

By T. STYLES

ARE YOU ON OUR EMAIL LIST?
SIGN UP ON OUR WEBSITE
www.thecartelpublications.com
OR TEXT THE WORD:
CARTELBOOKS TO 22828
FOR PRIZES, CONTESTS, ETC.

# CHECK OUT OTHER TITLES BY THE CARTEL PUBLICATIONS

By T. STYLES

WWW.THECARTELPUBLICATIONS.COM

# WAR 4:
# SKULL ISLAND
## By
## T. Styles

Library of Congress Control Number: 2019908144

ISBN 10: 1948373270

ISBN 13: 978-1948373272

Cover Design: Book Slut Girl

First Edition
Printed in the United States of America

What Up Fam,

Happy summer to you all! I hope this love note finds you well. I'm so excited with the new ventures we have coming for you! Starting with our Audio Books! We are finally converting our novels into Audio Book format. You guys have been asking and we heard you. So far we have eight of them up and running with more on the way so be on the lookout.

Also, T. Styles will be hosting her, **"BEST FRIEND IN A HANDBAG" PODCAST!** They will be available via ITunes and Google so make sure you go subscribe. She will be dropping behind the scenes tea on her stories and SO MUCH MORE!

Now, onto the book in hand, "WAR 4: SKULL ISLAND"...I    ABSO-FUCKIN_LUTELY...ADORED this novel! To say this is my favorite part may not be fair to the rest of the series, however, it may be my truth! But I'ma stop right there before I say too much and just let you read for yourselves.

With that being said, keeping in line with tradition, we want to give respect to a vet or new trailblazer paving the way. In this novel, we would like to recognize:

8                    By T. STYLES

# JESSICA 'LYRIC' ROBINSON

Jessica Robinson came to The Cartel Publications initially in 2007. She was one of our original Street Team members who was crucial in the launching of our publications company. Jessica went on to complete several novels of her own before becoming a nurse. Sadly, on May 21, 2019, we lost Jessica suddenly.

We are forever grateful for the love and dedication we received from Lyric and are blessed to have shared a tiny part of her world. We will always love you Jessica! R.I.P.

Aight, I've kept you longer than I should have...Goin' and get to it. I'll catch you in the next book.

Be Easy!

Charisse "C. Wash" Washington
Vice President
The Cartel Publications
**www.thecartelpublications.com**
www.facebook.com/publishercwash

Instagram: publishercwash
**www.twitter.com/cartelbooks**
**www.facebook.com/cartelpublications**
Follow us on Instagram: Cartelpublications
**#CartelPublications**
**#UrbanFiction**
**#PrayForCece**
**#RIPJessica**

# #War4

*Manipulation works well, until its power wears off and the captor becomes aware. My love, this is when the horror begins.*

*-- Bethany Wales*

# PROLOGUE
## JANUARY 1988

*I* t was frigid, but not enough to keep the bored from going outdoors.

*Wrapped in a Caucasian three quarter inch leather coat, fourteen-year-old Mason sat on the top step in front of his building. His portable radio blasted the hit song 'How Ya Like Me Now' by Kool Moe Dee.*

*And yet Mason had no time for moving to the beat. He was intense. Besides, a firm eye was necessary in the moment.*

*The firmest of eyes if anyone had asked.*

*After all he had been afforded the highest responsibility in the free land.*

*That of judge and jury.*

*"How I look now?" Blakeslee asked after doing her best Mason impersonation. The two French braids she was known for ran down her back. Her body cocooned in Mason's red and yellow 8 ball leather jacket, she was doing her best to keep warm.*

Mason crossed his arms over his chest making it obvious he wasn't impressed. "Nah. That ain't it."

"N...nah?" She repeated, feeling the swirling sensation of defeat in her gut. "But I...I mean...what am I doing wrong?" She wiped her cool forehead, forcing loose curls from the French braids, causing one hell of a tickle. At the same time, destroying any chance of looking boyish simply because she was so damn pretty.

"I 'on't know," Mason shrugged. "I mean, it's something like me but nothing like me."

Blakeslee was perplexed. How could she began to win Nikki back if she couldn't convince her that she wasn't some weird bull dagger, as she heard the term thrown around the city, if she couldn't walk like a real boy? How could she appeal to the inner most side of Nikki who was, well, straight?

With no interest in being with another girl.

Excluding those moments they shared in Blakeslee's bedroom, when both assumed no one was watching. Only later learning that Mason had seen them kissing, and took to snitching to Blakeslee's mother, resulting in Angie tossing Nikki out by her hair, ruining their bond.

Cocky above all else, Mason thought it was best to show her how to properly move like a guy. After all, he had ulterior motives. Maybe if Blakeslee could see how cool he himself was...maybe if she got a full whiff of his bad boy swag, then maybe, just maybe she would abandon all hopes of being male and surrender to him once and for all.

Rising off the cold step, he dusted his leather coat and took a few seconds to stare down at Blakeslee. He could feel her studying his every motion, hoping to not only emulate him but to become him.

Slowly he bopped down the steps taking several breaths for effect. Fog puffs rolled from his nostrils and floated above his head, before disappearing in the air. "Now you gotta pay attention. 'Cause for real, its like, like you not feeling me or somethin'."

"But I am feeling you," she said with her whole heart. "I, I just gotta work harder."

Mason moved closer wanting nothing more than to kiss her like she let him do that one time in his bedroom. The time they had sex. "Nah. Like really pay attention. Because if I gotta keep showing you the same thing, then I'ma start feeling like you not gonna be able to do it. Like maybe you should just let her go and—"

"I'ma get it," Blakeslee said grabbing his hand. Letting Nikki go was not an option and the world knew it. "Trust me."

All the bluster and arrogance he possessed suddenly diminished when he felt the warmth of her touch.

"I will prove to you that I can do it, Mason." Her body trembled anxiously. She needed her friend if there was the slightest chance of getting Nikki back. "I just need a little more help that's all. Can you show me again? Please?"

Mason nodded and squeezed her hand softly.

Feeling like Mason was reading her touch for more than desperation, she pulled away.

Now embarrassed that he was doing a bit too much, Mason cleared his throat. "Okay, okay, you gotta focus, because if we gonna get her boyfriend out the way, you gotta do everything right. You gotta make her believe you are me."

And then, in a manner too silly to be taken seriously, he paraded up the sidewalk with wide arms and wide strides like George Jefferson. In fact, as Blakeslee paid attention, she couldn't recall one time in her young life that she'd seen him walk so foolishly.

Still, Blakeslee was smart.

*Much smarter than most gave her credit for.*

*And she knew in her heart of hearts, if she was going to win over Nikki, Mason Louisville was the key.*

*She only prayed he wouldn't let her down.*

# CHAPTER ONE

You would have to see this splendid day on Wales Island to believe its beauty. The hue of the blue was definitive but for some reason the brilliance of the orange sun caused the sky to sparkle lightly. As if speckled with glitter dust.

And still, down below, a mysterious man that the world knew as Whoyawanmetabe, threw a monkey dick into paradise.

After all, why was he there?

Banks certainly hadn't invited him to the island. And sure Whoyawanmetabe had done jobs for Banks and Mason in America that placed them in his debt, but he assumed his payments would be of a monetary nature.

So what did the stranger want in his private place?

Eyes on the ocean, back faced Banks and Mason, he seemed to be transported somewhere else. Possibly the islands of Jamaica, far away from the tourist trap areas people liked to brag about when they visited the land.

Nah.

By T. STYLES

Deep on the island, where the sightseeing buses didn't roam, lie the heart and the hell of the country all at once. And it was in this place, that Whoyawanmetabe was born. Weighed with secrets and atrocities packed in his memories that would never allow him a good night's sleep.

Although enemies, Whoyawanmetabe, Banks and Mason were uniformed in all white linen, typical for island life.

"...But it was my aunt, who holds the most memories in my heart," Whoyawanmetabe continued, eyes still on the ocean, back still toward men who wanted to slice his neck if they thought their efforts would be final and he would go away forever. Instead, since he had exited his plane with ten men armed to the guilds, they had to remain steady.

"She used to make this coconut flavored sangria," Whoyawanmetabe continued. "To this day I haven't been able to find anyone who can come close to mastering the taste." He laughed to himself, his accent rich and thick with culture, although he didn't break sentences, traditional for some originating from Jamaica. His speech change perplexed Banks from the gate, because it showed that he moved as a man of many faces. "Would never give the..."

As he continued to ramble, Mason turned to look at Banks in frustration. "Give the word, and on God its off with his head," he whispered. "I mean look at the nigga. He got his back toward us and everything...begging us to kill him. Let me put him out his misery. Do it for Baltimore."

Banks glared at Mason. "Nah...he ain't the type you can just blow off." He focused on Whoyawanmetabe who was still talking, totally unbothered. "Something up with—"

"How come you hesitate when we have him in our sights?" Mason asked, low voice, clenched teeth. "I get that careful shit back home, but he's right here, Banks. The nigga's right here. Alone...with us. On your island. Let's dead him and be done with it once and for all."

Banks eyes narrowed into slits. "This man is connected," he whispered moving closer, to keep their scheming away from Whoyawanmetabe's eardrums. "To get rid of a bee infestation you don't cut down the hive. You'll get stung. You must—"

"Are you listening?" Whoyawanmetabe asked, turning his head toward the men.

Mason glared.

Banks nodded.

Whoyawanmetabe focused back on the ocean now that all the attention had been returned to its rightful place.

On him.

"It took me years to find out how she flavored the coconut. Some pieces were sweet and soft, others were rough but flavored to perfection."

"How she do it?" Banks asked, hoping the simplest of information would bring him closer to answers. No doubt, Mr. Wales was desperate beyond it all for the truth.

"Skin."

Mason frowned.

Banks shifted a little. "S...skin?"

Whoyawanmetabe smiled. "Yes. Used shaved skin from her palms to merge into the coconut." He turned around and walked up to the duo. "So that everyone drinking it would have a little bit of her soul. She was my first love. Truly. The first woman I wanted, but could never have. There was one other but she deserted me." He glared into space.

They were grossed the fuck out.

Mason shrugged. "Okay?" He didn't give a fuck. "What this got to do with us again?"

"Can you believe she was fifty at the time?"

"Your lady?" Banks asked.

"My aunt."

Banks' posture took on a rigid stance. Unlike the homie, he was willing to move slowly in an effort to discern what he didn't understand. At the same time, he was screaming inside and it caused his body to tense.

Yesterday he flew to Wales Island, with Mason and his sons, all of which Banks had been beefing with, only to learn that Whoyawanmetabe was there also. Add to his struggles the fact that his son Harris was murdered in prison, via a knife wound that Banks had sanctioned, in an effort to have him taken out of the facility to a hospital. Where the plan was to help him escape and hit it to the island. So patience was few and far between for Banks Wales.

"Did you...I mean, you said your aunt was your first love but did you...like..." Banks couldn't release the words because he was so disgusted.

"That's my little secret now ain't it?" Whoyawanmetabe said. "If I tell you I'd—"

"Nigga, what do you want with us?" Mason snapped, hands clapping together for each word. "You show up with a gang of bitch boys to a place off the grid and then you rapping about a aunt you probably fucked. What part of this has to do with why you here fucking with us? We ain't nothing but Bmore niggas."

Banks bit the inside of his lip. He wanted to go in on Mason on the spot, but Mason was a hair trigger, from day one. You had to be careful or it would be like throwing gasoline in the face of someone smoking a cigarette.

"I know you're anxious," Whoyawanmetabe said turning around to face him. "Almost as anxious as you were when you called, begging for me to get you out of jail."

"I didn't beg for—"

"And I came through...didn't I?" He continued cutting Mason off. "With no problems. As a result you're a free man...still on the run from the police maybe but able to be in such a beautiful place with your good friend." He looked at Banks.

Mason wiped his hand down his face, giving his chin a light squeeze upon hearing the truth.

"And what about you Banks? When you needed me to do the many things, which allowed you to go higher in the dope game. Was my presence an irritant then?"

"It was Nidia who—"

"Fuck that!" He beat his chest. "I was the one who parted the red streets for you, nigga...which allowed you power..." he stepped closer. "...To rise. You just didn't know. I kept more men away from your head than you realize Mr. Wales...if only you knew."

Mason glared. "But this is going too far now," Mason said.

"As far as I went when you called on me to plant a bomb in Banks' pilot friend's toilet so that you could—"

"I get all that," Mason interrupted. "You got the intel on both of us. So what you want? Money?"

He shook his head. "That's the trouble with American's. You think all debts can be paid with cash."

The muscles in Mason's arms twitched.

"We have a table full of food waiting." Whoyawanmetabe responded.

He touched both of them lightly on their arms and it was as if a painful electrical current ran through their bodies. They noticed something about him in the short time. He always liked to touch and smell things, as if doing so made them realer.

"Lets eat." Whoyawanmetabe said. "The time for understanding is near."

# CHAPTER TWO

The sky roof was open in the dining room, allowing the moonlight to shimmer against the Wales', Lou's and Whoyawanmetabe along with his crew, as they sat around the dinner table. With the Nunez family, the people charged with caring for the land, missing in action, the meal was not as elaborate as it had been in the past. However, Bet and Jersey did their best to make rice, beans, and flavored lamb to compliment whatever tragedy they knew was about to befall them.

The night called the best guests for the evening, including Banks, Mason, Jersey, Bet, Joey, Spacey, Minnie, Howard, Derrick, Patterson, Arlyndo and Shay. Along with the master of ceremonies, Whoyawanmetabe.

All were dressed in white.

As the candles held in candelabras flickered in the background, Whoyawanmetabe took the moment to wipe the corners of his mouth with a cream linen napkin, embroidered with the words THE WALES in gold. Although Banks occupied the head of the table, Whoyawanmetabe sat on the far opposite end of him.

Who was in charge?

The people wanted to know.

Everyone was silent as they watched Whoyawanmetabe pat the corners of his mouth repeatedly, despite not a food particle being upon his lips.

"Where I grew up, it was always about culture and family." He dropped the napkin into his lap. His accent a thing of the past. "So much so, that when we—"

"Where's your accent now?" Mason interrupted, drilling at his teeth with a toothpick. "Huh?"

"Excuse me?"

"It's just that sometimes you Jamaican, sometimes you British." The vein in Mason's neck bubbled with rage. "So tell me, who the fuck is you now? I mean really? You gotta pick a country or you a traitor if you ask me."

Banks' jaw twitched. One of the reasons he and Mason stayed at odds was because he didn't understand the importance of falling the fuck back and saying less. The man was intent on rattling the loose cages of lions.

Whoyawanmetabe grinned. "I'm fluent in over twenty languages. And although I am Jamaican, I spent my teenage years in London. So, forgive me if I revolve back and forth, I've earned the right."

Mason shifted a little in his seat and forked some rice into his mouth, despite not being hungry.

"I understand that you're anxious, but I'm a guest." Whoyawanmetabe continued. "And it is important to humor guests a little. So I urge you to fall back. It will be better for your health."

Catching the threat, Mason bit at the skin inside his cheek, tasting his own blood in the process.

"When I was coming up, it was just me, my mother and my aunt. Between the two of them they made sure I didn't want for anything." Whoyawanmetabe sat back in his seat, and grabbed his crystal and gold goblet filled with wine. "Now my mother was an adamant gardener but it was my aunt who inspired happiness. Whenever there was a party, they would come from all over my country, just to see her. The woman was a born star, kicking her thick legs

By T. STYLES

like a ballerina, flaring her arms like a composer in an opera...my aunt was simply amazing." His eyes grew large with excitement and for the moment he resembled a madman. Taking a deep breath he settled down. "And I always wondered one thing."

Banks shifted in his seat. The man's purpose for being there was near; he felt it in his heart.

"What would have happened if cameras had been following her at all times?" He sat up excitedly, as if finally all had been revealed. "Like on these stupid shows, except this time they would showcase someone worthy of the attention."

"I don't get it," Mason said. "Come harder."

"I want my cameras to follow both of your families." His smile was so wide and ridiculous, it was impossible to tell if he was being forthcoming or not. "I think this will be—"

"We not sitting in front of no fucking cameras," Mason said, his lips pinched together in a tight line. A firm fist slamming down on the table, rattling the crystal plates.

Banks touched Mason's arm before focusing on Whoyawanmetabe. "Listen...we appreciate everything you did for us back in Baltimore. We do. But we have a lot going on right now. A lot of shit has happened that we haven't come to terms with yet." He looked at Bet, whose face was as red as wine. "My son just died. My daughter was found in a ditch and I...I guess...we need to settle down a little first. As a family. Alone."

Minnie's head hung low and Shay rubbed her back softly.

"The last thing I want to do is subject them to any more pain right now," Banks continued.

"I understand," Whoyawanmetabe said with an extended hand. "I do. But you will do what I'm asking, or else your family will get even smaller." He smiled brightly. "So how about we talk about this again, what do you say, in about two days from now?"

# CHAPTER THREE

Lying on her side, in her bedroom, Bet's gaze fell on a magnificent painting of a happy black family on an island. It was acquired well before she met Banks, as she was a connoisseur of sorts when it came to procuring art. In a sense, she wondered if loving the portrayal so much was the reason she was on an island with her family right now.

The serenity of it all almost looked the same.

Did she pull this lifestyle into her existence?

But what about the happy part?

She'd lost a son, her marriage was in turmoil and Whoyawanmetabe wanted something that couldn't be placed into words. All she wanted was to close her eyes and sleep her life away. Not even the open windows, bringing with it the sound of the ocean washing up on the beach could quiet her wild thoughts.

"How are you?" Banks asked, his voice a soft whisper.

Bet turned around and smiled when she saw Banks standing in the doorway. He walked further into the room, crawled up behind her and kissed the back of her neck.

Trying to relax, he took a deep breath and exhaled the warmth brushing up against her nape.

"I'm fine," she sighed. "I just...I just...never mind."

Banks kissed her neck again. Normally harder on Bet, believing her to be weak, he was trying to allow her the space she needed to grieve.

About Harris.

And about the stranger.

"I know what you're going through, Bet and you're allowed to feel some kind of way. All this shit is...I mean...it's fucked up."

There was a knock at the door, destroying the moment like a hammer to a framed photo. "Come in," Bet said secretly wishing whoever there would disappear, so that she could have the rare moment alone with her husband.

It didn't happen.

The door opened and Shay appeared on the other side. Her presence on the island was definitely awkward. For starters, Banks had killed her father Stretch, who was also the biological father of all the Wales children.

When Banks and Bet decided to have kids, it was important that they find a man who resembled Banks, and Stretch was it. However, after the war with the Lou's kicked off, it was apparent that the reason for Banks murdering Stretch was a combination of him betraying Banks, by letting the secret go that he was the father of his kids and the weakness he displayed when stress wore him down.

And then there was Shay, the biological sister to all of Banks' kids as well as Harris' girlfriend. Banks had no idea that Harris would fall for Shay as a lover but it made sense, they spent too much time in the house together. When they finally learned that they were siblings, they wanted the bond still, while Banks was intent on destroying it.

After all, they were sister and brother.

And now with Harris murdered in prison, it meant Shay was alone. And he and his wife would be forced to take care of her.

"What is it, Shay?" Banks asked.

She wiped her wild curly brown hair out of her face. "I just wanted to know if I could get you two anything?"

Bet smiled and turned around, her body now facing Banks. "I'm fine, honey. But thank you anyway."

Shay nodded and walked out, closing the door behind herself.

"Banks, why is she here? We owe her nothing."

"You know why she's here." He paused, thinking about Stretch's death in his mind. "Her entire family's gone and she is the sister to our children. Ain't leave me much choice. Anyway, I'm more concerned about you right now."

She tilted her head. "I thought you never liked me to talk about my feelings. I thought—"

"I know you cry every night, Bet. And I, I understand. Harris is, he's..."

"Dead," she whispered completing his sentence. "It's hard for you to say he's gone too?"

"It is." He admitted. "Sometimes." He thought about his face and all the things he wanted to say. "I know you can't grieve right now, but I promise, I will get him out of our house. I just need to figure out what he wants first."

"But he told you already. Some stupid documentary."

"I don't believe him." He touched the side of her face and tucked her hair behind her ear. Her light cheek reddened at his caress. When Banks first left the island, he was cold and aloof but now he seemed attentive and to be honest she didn't know how to accept the change. "I have a plan that will—"

"I want this man out of my house." She glared cutting him off ruining the affection he was attempting to show.

"And I'm working on that."

"Are you? Because you can't even control Mason. I have three kids left, don't get them hurt because you take this as a joke. Give him what he wants and hopefully he'll leave us be."

Banks sat up in bed. "You know like I do that strangers rarely tell you what they want right away. I mean, I hear what he's asking but I don't believe him."

She wiped a hand down her face.

"Please, Bet, just...just let me handle this."

He moved toward the door.

"Banks."

He paused and faced her.

"If something happens, and another one of my children gets hurt, I'll—"

"Let me stop you right there," Banks walked back toward the bed. "I got a lot on my mind. And you do too, which I totally understand. After all, we lost a child. But please, don't, don't threaten me again."

"Or what? You won't talk to me?" She laughed. "You know, manipulation works well until it's power wears off and the captor becomes aware. My love, this is when the horror begins."

"So I'm holding you captive now?"

She rolled over. "Close the door when you leave. I require more rest."

"...And I don't care," Mason yelled at Jersey as they stood in the middle of one of the guest bedrooms they were staying in. "Besides, we can't fly off this island without Banks and even if we could, let's not forget that we're probably wanted over the cops you killed in the states."

Her eyes squinted as she looked down, rubbing her arms. It was as if he wanted her to be in a constant state of fear, always.

"I know you, Mason. I've known you longer than any other man in my life. And I can see in your eyes that you believe you can handle this alone. But I'm begging you to help me get our family out of here safely. And the best way to do that is to not handle things by yourself."

"You gonna have to trust me." He shrugged and dropped his shoulders heavily. "I know a lot of shit happened and—"

"Mason, please!" Jersey's spirit was in an uproar.

She rubbed the back of her neck and moved closer. All she wanted was for the first time ever, to be able to say the right thing to her husband, to get him to see things her way. At the same time she could tell he was off the hinges, and probably not in the best position to receive her advice.

"I think you need to talk to Banks because something tells me that this man is—"

"Shut up!" He yelled, throwing a flat palm in her face. "Just, just shut the fuck up! This not like how things are back home." His eyes squinted with hate. "I know niggas like Whoyawanmeta-whatever-his-fucking-name-is. They think they smarter than everybody when they not. So fall back and just trust me that—"

"But, Mason, there's something I have to tell you about—"

"Jersey," he grabbed both of her arms and squeezed tightly. "Just relax. I got our family. I got us." He walked away.

# CHAPTER FOUR

The windows were open in the living room and brought with them a cool and calming breeze.

And yet, Banks stood in the middle of the floor next to Mason, looking at the faces of the Lou's and the Wales'. There was something on his mind and Jersey and Bet sat close to one another, each bracing for the worst.

Howard and Derrick stood behind Mason while Patterson and Arlyndo sat next to Minnie and Shay. Spacey and Joey posted up next to the doorway, to ensure Whoyawanmetabe and his armed cameramen and crew, would not enter.

After all, this meeting was a private affair.

"We're going to do what he's asking," Banks said straight up.

Most gasped.

"What you mean we gonna do it?" Mason asked stepping closer. "This nigga show up without an invite and we play his game?" He pointed at the closed door with his hand. "Are you serious?"

Banks' eyes narrowed. "Mason, I'm not saying we get freaked the fuck out in front of his cameras. I'm just saying we play along until its inconvenient and—"

"It's inconvenient now, bruh!" Mason continued.

"You have to—"

"Nah, you gotta listen to me this time." Mason snapped, interrupting Banks. He took a deep breath and looked behind himself to be sure Whoyawanmetabe wasn't entering. "I say we divide up and attack him and his crew," he whispered. "At dinnertime. If we do it right he won't see us coming. He has about...what...ten people and the pilot they keep locked up. And how many of us is it?"

"They took our weapons."

"But we got a couple guns," Mason continued.

"They took all our weapons," Banks repeated. "Even the ones you snuck in."

Mason was shocked, believing he hid them so well.

"Daddy, I'm scared," Minnie said looking over at Banks.

Banks stepped closer and placed a soft hand on the side of her face. "You ain't gotta be scared

By T. STYLES

of nothing," he assured her. "All this Mason talking about ain't going down. We gonna take our time and—"

"That's your problem, you always wanna take your time when some moves need to be executed swiftly."

"Yeah, I'm not feeling moving slow either, Unc," Howard said.

"I think we hit the Jamaican first and his crew next," Derrick added. Although shot last year by Stretch in his lower region, he was better now and moving about without a wheelchair or cane.

"And then what?" Banks paused before looking at all of the Lou's. "Wait for someone else to come looking for him? On the island? Assuming I can get to my plane and get us out in time? The problem is we don't know shit about him!" He said, slamming his fist into his hand. "I know he's here for something else."

"I think he's—"

"Be quiet," Mason told Jersey, cutting her off. "Once we get rid of him and the camera flunkies, we can move for his pilot. They got him posted up right now with a man watching the door."

"Pops is right," Spacey said clearing his throat. "Just the fact that he drops and uses his accent at will, lets me know something is strange. We should chill."

Howard smirked and chuckled. "Still call him pops huh?"

Spacey frowned. "Fuck that supposed to mean?"

Howard grinned. "I think every nigga in here know what the fuck I'm talking about by now. At this point, it ain't even a secret no more."

"Howard!" Jersey yelled sitting up.

"What, ma?" He shrugged. "We still playing the pretend game or are we gonna give any thought to the fact that Banks lied to all of us? By faking like a man when he a woman?"

Banks rushed up on Howard so fast he flinched. "This my house, lil nigga. And the day you forget, it'll be your last night here. Are we clear?"

Howard looked to his family for support but found himself lacking. "Dad, you gonna let this—"

"Mr. Wales," a woman said softly entering the unwatched doorway. The fellas were so in tuned with what was happening with Banks and Howard that they left the door unmanned.

Banks turned around, immediately shocked to see Rosa Nunez, along with her family, which included her daughters Cassandra, Emetine, Roxana, her son Tobias and her husband Ives. Originally there to take care of the home, he was surprised to learn that so much had occurred during his time in the states.

For instance, the last time Bet saw them, the Nunez family were trying to get to her through the reinforced door of Banks' lab. Because earlier that day, Bet had jammed a knife into her oldest daughter, Oswalda, killing her within minutes. When Bet and Joey finally came out of the lab, the family was gone and Banks was home.

That was four days ago. As far as the Wales family knew, the Nunez family was never coming back.

And yet, there they were.

But were they seeking revenge?

"What are you doing here?" Bet asked walking next to Banks, eyes firmly on the Nunez family for protection. "You aren't welcome anymore. Especially after everything that happened."

Rosa walked up slowly to Banks and Bet but Joey and Spacey blocked her path. She appeared meek and without any intent for ill will. "Mr. Wales, and Mrs. Wales, we didn't mean to leave in such a hurry but I, I had to bury my daughter." Her Spanish accent was thick. "It's tradition to bury your children within twenty-four hours after they die. The ceremony is sacred because we have to wash the body, pray over it and—"

"I don't give a fuck!" Bet yelled, her body trembling with rage. "You scared me. You, you took, took, took me to a place that...that I'm..." As her speech began to unravel Banks tried desperately to calm her down by pulling her closer toward his body.

"I wonder if you'll ever say I don't give a fuck about somebody you love." Rosa said.

Bet blinked several times.

"And you took my daughter away," Rosa continued, sobbing. "Don't I deserve to be a little angry too?"

"Bet, maybe things weren't as bad as they appeared," Banks said looking down at his wife. "A lot happened and you said it yourself that you were on edge about me being away and—"

"Nah, Pops," Joey interrupted. "I was here too. And it was just like ma said." He took a deep breath. "They were more than angry, I felt like they...like they were trying to hurt us. Maybe even kill us."

Banks looked back at the Nunez clan. "You can stay here for a week, until you find another place, but after that you and your family must go," he told Rosa. Looking at his wife he said, "Just trust me."

She nodded. "I understand. And, thank you." She turned around and looked at her family. They all walked out.

Bet moved around to face Banks and smacked him.

Her children pulled her back, but it was too late.

The havoc had already been started.

"One of these days you're going to regret not listening to me." Bet said, before storming away.

# CHAPTER FIVE

It was dinnertime but no one was hungry.

The Wales and Nunez family sat around the dining room table, all waiting to see what Banks, who stood at the helm, had to say. Would he rescue them from the obvious peril they were preparing to take with the island stranger?

Also in attendance were Whoyawanmetabe and his henchmen who hung along the walls. Their presence stated clearly that they were in charge.

Banks would have spoken his mind off top instead of waiting, but where were the Lou's? He needed all to be in the room and all to accept what he considered law.

Tiring of the delay, Banks took a deep breath, looked behind him at the entrance once more and back ahead at the islander's face. He knew whatever he was about to utter would impact everyone. Even the Nunez's wanted to leave after learning of the stranger with an even stranger request, but Whoyawanmetabe forced them to stay, only being able to walk about the few feet and beach surrounding the property.

Whoyawanmetabe strolled to the opposite end of the table, across from Banks and sat down. His fingertips brushed the shoulders of everyone he came near before he took a seat. "Are you prepared to tell me your answer?"

Banks looked at his wife, his children and the man. "I've decided that we will—"

"Let you live if you pack your shit and fly out tonight," Mason said, entering the dining room with Arlyndo, Howard, Patterson, Derrick and Jersey falling behind him like a linked chain.

The look on Jersey's face proved she was not a part of whatever show Mason had prepared. Derrick was also not feeling his father's energy but in a sense he was wearing a Lou jersey and had to go with the team.

Irritated at his antics, Whoyawanmetabe glared at Mason as if he was a petulant child, undeserving of his time or attention. "So what were you saying, Banks?"

"I was talking, not him," Mason grabbed his crotch and grinned. "We not having none of whatever you think you got going on here. What we want you to do is pack your shit and get the fuck off Wales Island. What part of that don't you get, my nigga?"

Whoyawanmetabe sat back, turned his head and chuckled once into his palm. It was apparent he had no respect for the man. Clearing his throat he said, "Does he speak for the majority?" His question was for all but his gaze rested on Banks.

The leader.

And as Banks thought about the inquiry, he was wrestling with a lot in the moment. He had a mad man on each side. One he loved like a brother and the other who came with mystery.

Why did his friend force him into such a precarious position? It was as if Mason loved drama above peace. The anger boiled so hard that his temple throbbed causing the blue veins in his forehead to bulge. At the same time he knew Mason's heart was in the right place, even if his brain was nowhere to be found.

"Banks, does he speak for the majority?" Whoyawanmetabe continued.

"We want you gone," Banks admitted. "This is true." Of course he wasn't going to say those words initially. He had planned to go with the flow. But he tried to side with the man he knew all his life instead.

Whoyawanmetabe pushed his chair back hard, causing the legs to scratch across the floor. Everyone but Banks and the Lou's buckled at his abrupt move.

Slowly he rose and although he was somewhat tall, about 6'2 to be exact, when he ascended from his chair, it was as if his head would brush the ceiling. The man was larger than life in the moment.

Taking a look at each person, he leisurely walked around the table. The air felt suddenly chilly and the women trembled with fear as he gently touched Bet's shoulder. Banks moved to jaw drop him upon the disrespect but was stopped by Whoyawanmetabe's goons. A man on each side of him penned him to the chair like a seat cushion.

After rousing Banks' emotions, Whoyawanmetabe moved toward Minnie and Banks was once again angered to the point of blacking out. He wiggled himself so much the men holding him vibrated violently like a dryer packed too deep, despite maintaining their hold.

It was clear Whoyawanmetabe wasn't taking a simple stroll.

He was selecting his prey.

"What you doing?" Mason asked sensing things had heated up to another level due to him. His arms folded against his chest and then dropped at his sides. "If you wanted to say something you could've said it from your seat."

Ignoring Mason, finally Whoyawanmetabe moved toward Emetine. "What you mean what am I doing?" He stood behind Emetine and stroked her shoulders like a lover before sniffing her hair, inhaling deeply. Her eyes glassed over as tears poured down her cheeks.

She had every right to be afraid.

"Stop playing games!" Mason was desperately trying to gain control where he had none. "You leaving the island or not?"

"You made a comment and I..." his hands moved quickly toward Emetine's throat and with one jolting motion he broke her neck. Her head hung loosely to the side before she slid out the chair, flopping on the floor like a weighted duffle bag.

Rosa fainted and Tobias moved to hurt Whoyawanmetabe before being knocked out cold by one of his goons.

The women screamed and everyone backed away from the table and from Whoyawanmetabe, whose henchmen had released Banks and grabbed the rest of the Nunez family since they, alone, experienced the loss.

"This is not a game," Whoyawanmetabe said loudly, his voice rocking all around. "And by now you know how serious I am. Now you have a glimpse of what I'm willing to do, to get what I want." He took a deep breath. "You will give me what I'm requesting or every man in this room will die."

Rosa sat on the edge of the bed, shivering at what she just witnessed. Although devastated, her cries ceased long ago. Her throat raw and bloodied due to straining her vocal cords. Her family, Tobias, Cassandra and Ives...all stood in front of her, wishing they could take back what they never foresaw happening.

Mentally insane, Roxana, her youngest, was on the floor trembling. She would have to drug her sleep until Whoyawanmetabe left because her mood swings were reckless.

"When we first came here, when he hired us to take care of this place," Rosa said in her native language, "I knew in my spirit that we shouldn't have come. I knew that we shouldn't be here...but...but I allowed him to guide me because I wanted...I wanted..." she cried harder.

Ives, her husband, rushed up to soothe her. "Don't worry we will be—"

"Get away from me you coward!" She yelled. "Just, just get away." Her voice was husky and she grabbed a tissue, dabbing the inside of her mouth as blood appeared before her eyes.

Slowly he rose and rejoined the line with his children. "But, what can I, what can I do?" Ives asked.

"You could've fought for me. You could've fought for us. Instead, you stand by and watch as two of our girls were taken while you sit in your room all day watching child pornography!"

He glared, looked at his spawn and back at her in shame. "It's not child porn! They're young women who—"

"About the same age of your daughters!" Rosa snapped. "That makes it right to you?" She tossed the bloody tissue on the bed and massaged her sore throat. "Before they came we didn't use their tech and now look, they are tearing us apart with their evil ways before *he* even returns."

Ives rocked a little. "But, there was, I mean, how was I to know he would hurt her, Rosa?" He trembled. "And Oswalda was murdered by Mrs. Wales when I wasn't home. It's not my—"

"You are not a man, Ives," she said, finding it hard to talk due to the pain in her throat. "And I should have never married you."

"Ma, this hurts all of us," Tobias said, his eye blackened due to the blow from Whoyawanmetabe's goon. "Don't blame dad. He couldn't do anything."

"Yeah, mom," Cassandra added. "It's not his fault. The Wales' and Lou's are to blame." Hate was on her tongue when she thought of the Americans.

"All I know is this, when he returns the Wales' and that Jamaican will pay for what they have done to my family. And it will be the most pain they've ever experienced in their lives. I can guarantee it."

"I don't give a fuck!" Banks roared at Mason as they stood on the beach, their feet sinking into the warm sand. "Look what just happened!" He pointed at the house. "The nigga killed an innocent girl all because you can't fall the fuck back. Even though I begged you to!"

"I get that."

"Then how come it sounds like you don't care?"

Mason wiped his hand down his face. "I mean, what Banks, at least it wasn't one of our kids." He threw his arms at his sides and they fell heavily.

Upon hearing his words, Banks was a new brand of heated. "This not a fucking game!" He yelled rushing up to him. "It wasn't one of ours but could've been. And because of your temper, I could've lost another child tonight."

"Shit gonna be fine, Banks."

"Nah, it won't be fine...I will never forgive you for this shit. Ever!" He stormed away.

# CHAPTER SIX

*I*t was chilly but comfortable as Blakeslee stood outside of her school. When she was ready, she took a deep breath and approached Nikki as she strutted out of the building, a wide smile on her face.

*For a second, Blakeslee paused and took in her carefree expression. It made her look as if everything great was going on in her world. Didn't she miss Blakeslee as much as she missed her? Didn't she want their friendship as much as Blakeslee did? She didn't want her sad but once, just once, she wanted Nikki to at least look as if she was on her mind.*

*This meeting was a bit overdue. Blakeslee had seen her in the hallway earlier but couldn't build up the courage to speak. So she waited for her to come outside instead. Still, she hoped that with a little time and the right words, she was now ready to approach.*

*Luckily for her, the homie, Mason, wasn't too far away, as usual. He made it his life's mission to always be on hand to rescue Blakeslee if she needed him. And yet Mason still held onto hope.*

That maybe, one day soon, he could convince his true love that being a boy was a worthless chore. That being with him was best for all parties concerned.

But that was the future.

For now the moment was all about the walk.

A walk Blakeslee studied to great accord.

A walk that Mason had worked tirelessly to help her perfect, in an attempt to make her look as foolish as possible in the eyes of Nikki. And as he stood from a far watching, he mumbled a phrase repeatedly as if it were an omen.

"Please don't work...please don't work...please don't work." Mason chanted.

Taking a deep breath, Blakeslee bopped toward Nikki foolishly just as her new boyfriend Hector bolted out the door.

Blakeslee stopped in her tracks.

"Aye, Nik!"

Nikki turned around and smiled when she saw his face. The smile went on forever as they stared at one another with admiration and appreciation. It was then that Blakeslee noticed she was even wearing his leather jacket.

Blakeslee was crushed.

*One of the reasons she found it hard to start a friendship with Nikki was because Hector was always there.*

*Waiting.*

*Hovering.*

*Protecting.*

*If you knew the history you'd understand why he was so diligent. He wanted her from the gate, back in the day when Nikki was running with Mason and Blakeslee. But the beautiful girl was always too busy for him. Still, he was relentless. Since his father was a pimp, he learned that with a woman all you had to do was be available.*

*To wait.*

*And if you were patient enough, and occupied by other females of course, in time, the one you want would always come your way.*

*And he was right.*

*He stayed the course and eventually the trio was dismantled due to 'the kiss' and Nikki was alone. In a sense he was what they referred to as 'a nigga in wait' and he was quite alright with that title. Besides, every bad bitch worth her salt had one.*

As Blakeslee saw Hector drape his arm around her neck as they walked, she felt it was a losing battle. And then she heard...

"Aye, Hector, let me holla at you right quick!"

When Blakeslee turned around, she smiled when she saw Mason putting the firm block on the 'boyfriend-girlfriend' scenario. By wanting to separate Hector from Nikki in Blakeslee's name.

Hector, who was all too eager to be a part of Mason's crew, damn near knocked Nikki in the face as he ripped his arm from her neck, in an attempt to be on the ready for Mason.

A move that bought Blakeslee a little time to kick her game, which was in early development. "Nikki," Blakeslee said, swallowing the lump in her throat. "How you...like...what you—"

"Why you walk over here like that?" She looked her up and down.

Blakeslee's mouth opened and closed heavily. She had studied Mason's gait so hard, only to look like a fool.

"Listen, I don't wanna talk to you," she said rolling her eyes. "I already told you that, dang." She squeezed her books closer to her chest, as if protecting her heart. "I wish you just leave me alone. I mean, how many times I gotta tell you I got a boyfriend?"

"All I wanna be is your friend though," she said, although secretly hoping for more. "We don't talk like we—"

"Well Hector don't got female friends and he don't want me having any male ones."

Blakeslee smiled. Did she see her as a boy already?

"I'm talking about Mason," Nikki continued, destroying her happiness that quickly. "I know you a girl."

Blakeslee looked down and kicked a few rocks. "Why we can't be friends though?"

Nikki sighed deeply and tucked her long hair behind her ear. "Because you...you..." She took a deep breath.

Truth be told, Nikki didn't know why Hector didn't want her befriending Blakeslee. At the end of the day she didn't care. Hector was considered a bun (a cutie pie) with his Black and Hispanic heritage and all the girls wanted him but luckily for her, he wanted her instead.

Looking for a place to put blame for why she wanted to ignore Blakeslee, Nikki judged her boyish clothing, which fell off her frame and made her look more silly than masculine. "...Why you dressed like that anyway? You look stupid."

Blakeslee looked down at her large jeans and oversized shirt that belonged to her father. Not only did she fail desperately at being a 'boy', her father's current financial situation couldn't afford her a better chance even if she tried harder.

"I...I wanted to look nice for you. So—"

"Look, we can't be friends okay?" Nikki said firmly, failing to wait for an answer.

"But if you would, like, if you could give me a good reason I could...I mean—"

"Everything good over here?" Hector asked rejoining his girl, a heavy arm around her neck again.

Mason had held him at bay as long as possible.

"Everything's great now," Nikki said grinning up at him.

Hector rolled his eyes at Blakeslee. "Well let's go get some wings with mumbo." He said to his girl. "I'm hungry." They walked away, leaving Blakeslee broken hearted.

Mason quickly rejoined his friend. "You good?"

"No," she said honestly, her eyes already watering.

*"Well you gonna be better tonight."*

*Blakeslee frowned. Her mind trying to imagine which scenario could take her from feeling like shit sliding out of a dog's ass, to better. "Why you say that?"*

*"He coming to my party."*

*"Who? Hector?"*

*"Yep, and I told him to leave his girl at home."*

*Blakeslee tucked her hands in the tattered coat pockets she was wearing. "He, he agreed to do that?"*

*"After I told him other girls would be there, he ain't think nothing about it," He said in a flat voice. "He wanna hump something I guess. The nigga Hector a freak. All the bitches know."*

*Blakeslee's jaw twitched.*

*She was mad that Hector was playing Nikki so inconsiderately, and that he was willing to leave her for the freaks Mason rolled with. But what could she do? Up until that moment Mason had always gotten her out of a bind.*

*He always saved the day.*

*Why should it change now?*

*The party was fire.*

*Mason had more girls than boys at his event, something he always planned. His father was out of town over night, to pick up cocaine from Nidia and didn't mind leaving him with the babysitter who only came by to let Mason 'kiss her special place' due to being the child pedophile that she was, along with his uncle.*

*So basically he was alone.*

*Everyone was dancing to the 80s hits except Blakeslee. She stood in the corner, wearing a dingy white t-shirt and blue jeans, her hair pulled back in a ponytail because her father couldn't afford someone to braid it, which Mason loved. Mainly because when her hair was pushed back it always placed her beauty on shine, despite the 'Dom-ness-tivity' that she was trying to possess.*

*On the opposite end of the spectrum, surrounded by three girls, Mason attempted to look as if he was having the time of his life but it wasn't working. He couldn't keep his eyes off Blakeslee. Wanting to be with her and dancing to the music.*

*Oh how he wished she wasn't so fucking pretty. How he wished he could hate her, and not be used to get who she truly wanted...Nikki. Why couldn't he lose count of the nights he pictured her face in his mind, and how the curls surrounding her angelic face would always find a way to wiggle out of her braids?*

*The boy was in love.*

*Point. Blank. Period.*

*Bolting from the throng of girls who fought for his attention, Mason found his way in front of tomboyish Blakeslee Wales instead. "Why you over here by yourself?"*

*Blakeslee shrugged.*

*"You wanna dance?" Mason asked, tucking his hands into his brand new jeans.*

*She frowned as if he were an oozing pimple on a nose. "Come on, Mason, you know I'm not 'bout to dance with you. It's not like—"*

*"Not with me," Mason said, interrupting her. "You thought I meant with me?" He pointed to himself.*

*Silence.*

They looked away from each other in embarrassment until Mason looked at her again. "So, you not gonna have no fun? You gonna sit here and—"

"Where Hector?"

He shrugged. "He here."

"Where though?"

"In the back. With some girls."

Blakeslee was so heated her light skin reddened. "I mean, why she wanna be with somebody who treat her so bad? He don't deserve her."

*And she don't deserve you.* Mason thought to himself.

"Let me go check and see what he doing right quick." Mason strutted toward the room in the back of the apartment. He gave Blakeslee a speech but the truth was he knew exactly what Hector was doing...finger fucking a girl from the block.

When Mason walked into his room, he saw a huge sheet covered bump on the bed, in the darkness. "Having fun?" Mason grinned from the doorway.

Slightly annoyed, Hector peeped his head from up under the sheet, the girl's face still concealed.

Her box braids dangling. "You know it," Hector smiled. "But close the door though."

Mason nodded and walked out.

Having seen all he needed to, he hit it back to tell his best friend that he was in possession of enough information to destroy Nikki's relationship for good. At the same time, he had to be careful. Would giving Blakeslee the intel actually destroy Nikki and Hector's relationship, which he really didn't want? Or would Mason come out like a hero for saving Blakeslee again by giving her the secret to get what she desired?

Mason held all the power.

He just needed to see how it would benefit him first.

# CHAPTER SEVEN

Minnie sat in the hot tub inside the mansion trying to soak away her tears with Shay, who was equally rocked by what transpired in the dining room.

They actually saw a woman's neck break like a twig.

It was an atrocity at best.

Both young women assumed life would be somewhat easier. Neither didn't have any firm expectations, but no one couldn't imagine so much misery in such a beautiful place.

Minnie was beside herself. It hadn't even been a week and already she learned her brother was dead and both had seen someone get murdered before their eyes.

They were still talking and trying to get their minds around Whoyawanmetabe's evil energy, when Tobias walked into the pool house wearing black swim trunks.

Shay saw how her sister friend looked at the man and so she eased out of the hot tub and grabbed her towel. "I'm going to study my books, Minnie." She wiped her tears away.

Minnie nodded.

Shay approached Tobias. "Sorry about your sister."

He smiled and she walked away.

Minnie thought about leaving too but something about the stranger intrigued her. Not that she was in the market for a new boyfriend, but still.

Before the homicide, she saw him across the dining room table, and briefly mentioned to herself how fine he was. Unfortunately the thought quickly exited after witnessing a murder.

"You mind if I get in with you?" He asked in his heavy accent. "I mean, I can come back later if—"

"No!" She cleared her throat. She sounded jive extra and had to calm herself to avoid looking anymore desperate. "I mean, you're welcome to stay. Plenty of room."

He slid into the hot tub and took a deep breath. "My name is Tobias." He extended his hand. "Yours?"

"Not interested."

He dropped his hand. "I wasn't trying to come on to you. I just wanted...just wanted to introduce myself. Maybe make a little small talk to get my mind off of watching my sister get killed. As if that's possible."

Minnie immediately felt like shit. She knew she had a nasty way about her mouth and although she had meant to be kinder, wanting and doing were two different things.

She extended her hand slowly. "I'm Minnie. Minnesota Wales."

He waded through the water to shake her hand and the instant their fingers connected, there was an immediate attraction, although both knew it was neither the time nor the place to explore the moment.

"I'm sorry about your sister," she said honestly emerging deeper into the hot tub, allowing the bubbles to caress her collarbone.

"Me too." He lowered his head although his breath increased as he battled with how to suppress the rage to kill everything and everybody. "My mother and father burying her now."

Minnie nodded having heard the brief story on how Bet had murdered Oswalda in the kitchen. There wasn't much time to explore the topic, because she had to deal with Harris being dead too, but she knew enough to realize that her family was responsible for this man's misery.

"My mother, when she did whatever she did, she wasn't in her right mind. At least I don't think so."

"Whatever she did?" he repeated. "She killed my sister. That's a fact."

"I didn't mean it that way. I...I mean...if we're going to get to know each other, since we're forced to be here, you'll learn that sometimes I say the opposite of what I mean...I mean...my mother is sick. I always knew it, based on the strange things she used to do around the house but I guess, I mean, I guess we all tried to suppress it. There's no hiding it now. And I am sorry about your sister. My father is too."

He took another full breath. "I never show much emotion." He said. "I find it useless anyway, but since Oswalda died, I never got a chance to reconcile with losing her you know? And now with Emetine I'm...I'm confused. Felt like I could've done something."

70

"You tried to," she said.

"I feel the same. My brother was murdered recently. It's like you have people around you and don't know the importance of having them until they aren't here anymore. If I had known, if I had any idea that I wouldn't see my brother again I would've hugged him. Told him how I feel but now..."

He nodded in agreement and sunk deeper into the hot tub. "You're wise. To be so young."

"How you know my age?"

"Fifteen or sixteen right?"

"Sixteen...and a half." She did her best to boost her age and her chances with him unconsciously.

He laughed quietly, saw his sisters' faces in his mind and his expression carried the weight of extreme sadness and guilt. There was nothing to be happy about. Nothing to smile about either.

"Are you okay?" She asked softly.

"I will be."

She nodded. "So tell me about this island. How big is it?"

"Your property is about fifty miles wide all way around but toward the east it connects to another much larger island. You have to drive over a wooden rocky road to get there but even if you could you wouldn't want to."

"Why?"

"Not everybody is excited about having outsiders here. Some people are, well, upset."

"Is that where you and your family went? When you left."

"We buried our sister over there...but since we can't leave...I mean we like it much better anyway so Emetine will rest here. It feels like home."

"But it shouldn't feel like home," Bet said entering the pool house. Having an unrequited crush on Tobias, she didn't take too kindly to him being so close to her daughter. He on the other hand, despised Bet, especially after entering the kitchen minutes after Bet killed Oswalda.

"Mrs. Wales," he said through clenched teeth in an attempt to show respect for a woman he despised. The hate was apparent.

"Leave us alone, Tobias." Bet demanded.

He nodded, exited the hot tub and grabbed a towel.

On the way out of the pool house, he ran into Arlyndo in the hallway.

"I don't know who you are but that girl isn't available." Arlyndo said.

Tobias found the boy amusing. He hadn't been around the Lou's long, but he observed enough to know they were the reverse of the Wales family. Like weird doppelgangers. Lacking class and couth.

"My sister just died and—"

"I don't give a fuck about that bitch." He pointed at the floor. "Stay away from Minnie."

Tobias dabbed his face with the towel. He looked down and slowly his eyes met Arlyndo's. "You're like your father."

"Fuck that supposed to mean?"

"You lack self control. That's gonna get you in trouble in the near future."

"What that got to do with me and my girl?"

"If I want her, you'll know. But for now you're good so relax." Tobias attempted to walk away when Arlyndo grabbed his arm; sharp nails digging into his flesh.

"I went through a lot to get her back. For your sake don't get in my way." He released him and Tobias walked down the hall, smiling all the way.

"Ma, I wasn't trying to be fresh with him," Minnie said as she shared the hot tub with Bet. "So stop saying that. He was being nice and—"

"It's not about being nice. It's about so much more. That family has ulterior motives and with Whoyawanmetabe roaming around, we can't be sure about the Nunez family's intentions. He is very dangerous and I'm trying to explain it to your father. What if the Nunez's and him work together to kill us?"

"Mother...what really happen the night you murdered that girl?"

Bet looked away. "I can't explain it...she was...she was...tormenting me. As if she could, read my mind or something. And I realize this sounds odd. Whenever I talk about it your father, you kids, nobody believes me. It's like, she would be around, filling my head with the wildest thoughts, even in my sleep." She sat back. "And what does your father go do? Invite them to stay longer. Stupid, man!"

She frowned. "Maybe that was on purpose."

Bet's eyes squinted. "What does that mean?"

"If the Nunez family hadn't been here, maybe he would have broken your neck instead. Or mine. Or Shay's." She paused. "Uncle Mason was always gonna fight back. So I'm glad Pops let them back even though I feel bad."

"Minnie, you have no idea what you're talking about."

"True, I wasn't here for what you went through, ma, but dad is smart and—"

"You so easily still refer to him as daddy." Bet said, her expression crooked and connected to malice. "That's nice." Her eyes were wide and wild.

"But he is my father."

"Technically he's your mother but...who cares about titles."

Minnie glared. "You both worked so hard to get us to follow the family rules and now you want me to change?"

"I don't want you to change and you bet not tell Banks that either!" She yelled, eyes wild and crazy. "I just want somebody in this damn family to remember that, that man left me and Joey on this island alone. And when he comes back he brings the Lou's with him! What about me?"

Minnie nodded although this was another glimpse into the picture that maybe her mother was mentally sick and worse, completely unhinged.

"Are you, are you better now, ma?"

Bet soaked deeper into the hot tub and closed her eyes.

# CHAPTER EIGHT

The sun shined behind Banks as he met with the Lou's, Wales and Nunez families in the living room. After Emetine's murder there was no mistaking the severity of what they were dealing with when it came to Whoyawanmetabe. The approach had to be smooth to avoid further casualties since they were out gunned and out manned.

Whoyawanmetabe was ruthless.

And to prevent the family from leaving Wales Island and crossing over into the larger connecting island, Whoyawanmetabe's men did tours on the raggedy bridge leading to the adjacent land.

They were all hostage.

Mason and his sons had taken down their vigor several notches after Emetine's murder, although they were still ready to attack if Banks gave the word.

With a bowed head Banks said, "We gonna do this. We need to give him what he wants."

Many sighed but they already knew the choice was not their own.

"What does this mean, Banks?" Jersey asked softly, clutching Bet's hand so hard her fingertips ran blue. "I understand we must comply I'm just...I need to know what are we supposed to do for him?"

Banks tugged at his shirt's hem and looked at her with lifeless eyes. "They will follow us around with their cameras. Basically taping all aspects of our lives. It sounds harmless enough." He didn't believe his own words.

"So we gotta worry about these niggas taping us while we sleep too?" Mason asked. His voice alone irritated Banks.

"No, I told him when we're in our rooms the cameras are off limits."

Mason chuckled. "And let me guess, you believe him?"

Banks' neck corded as he tensed up. "We don't have a choice. Even if we think something else is going on, even if we know there's another reason he's here, we have to fake like we're clueless at this point. Because..." He ran his hand down his chin. "...We are."

"So, daddy, should we put on a show?" Minnie asked softly.

"Like the real housewives of—"

"No," Banks said, cutting Shay off abruptly to stop the stupidity at the door.

"Well like Minnie said, if we can do a little more, maybe we can get them out of here sooner," Tobias responded, his eyes red and black from stress and being knocked out.

"Well don't do too much," Arlyndo glared at him from across the room. "You could hurt yourself, my nigga."

Tobias smiled. "I'm Latino."

Arlyndo's jaw twitched.

"I don't see anything wrong with giving them a little show, but you have to be careful," Banks warned. "This man is way smarter than he appears. Follow the line to your emotions, to what you really feel in the moment, and if you can add a little more to make it good for filming do that. But I don't want our families more damaged than they already are trying to appease him."

"Man, I can't believe we going through with this shit," Mason said shaking his head. "This dude got us performing like circus clowns. I mean, what the fuck is really going on?"

Banks looked at him. "We staying alive. Besides, we tried your way, remember? And what happened?"

Everyone looked at the Nunez family who was shooting visual daggers Mason's way.

"You ain't gotta remind me."

"You sure?" Banks asked moving closer to him. "Because the look in your eyes tell me you still ain't getting it." He pointed in his face. "It's making me think you still believe this is all a game."

Mason smirked at Banks as if he were his worst enemy. "I'm out." The entire Louisville family rose and followed Mason through the door.

Banks took a deep breath and looked at his family and the Nunez's. "Be easy with this entire situation, until I figure things out. Okay? That's all I'm asking."

Banks and Whoyawanmetabe sat in the lounge; both had whiskey glasses in hand. Although it was not cold out, Banks enjoyed the fireplace and so it crackled, casting soft orange glows on their faces.

"They're going to do it," Banks said taking a sip before placing the glass on the table. It clanked lightly.

Whoyawanmetabe smiled in pleasure, although it wasn't as if any of the three families had much say in the matter. "This is good, for all parties involved. And it makes me really happy."

"What are you doing with the footage? I mean a few niggas in Baltimore know us but other than that, not many people will be interested in what we do in our day to day lives."

"You underestimate yourselves. You're very popular in—"

"I'm serious." Banks said firmly, fists clenched in his lap.

Whoyawanmetabe took a large sip and sat back until the butter soft leather cushions imprinted with the weight of his body. "I have my reasons for the footage. And not everything is for everybody."

"You have to be showing this to someone. You want it too badly."

"You see, that's the assumption with most Americans. You wear jewelry for other people instead of simply cherishing the precious metals or diamonds that make up these ornaments. You buy cars hoping someone else will see you in them instead of enjoying the comfort they provide while traveling."

"What does this mean for me and my family?" Banks asked through clenched teeth, doing his best to keep his composure. "I'm tired of the riddles. The talking around what I'm asking. Speak in specifics. Because I don't give a fuck about none of that other shit you saying."

Whoyawanmetabe nodded. "I am a very rich man. And unfortunately, my violent lifestyle means I'll never have a family of my own. Which means I won't be able to see the inner workings of them on a private level. Ever, and I desperately crave to witness real human interactions. I desperately crave to witness real human love. For me the Wales', Lou's and even the Nunez's will provide this."

He was lying and Banks was certain.

"You sure the objective isn't to destroy us?"

"Can you be destroyed?" He paused. "You know, I dated a girl in Jamaica who used to read a book called *A Course In Miracles*. There was one passage she kept quoting. *'Nothing real can be threatened. Nothing unreal exists.'*"

Banks readjusted and picked up his glass, taking another sip to avoid showing his angry disposition.

"So if your love is real nothing can threaten it, Mr. Wales."

"You talk as if you're not human." Banks readjusted in his seat.

"In most circles, I've been labeled a monster."

Banks sat back. "Are you?"

"Mr. Wales, all I can say is that these recordings will not leave my possession. And when I travel or go about, I'll think of your family, the Lou's and the Nunez's while watching them. It'll be like I'm a part of your family unit."

"Why don't I believe you?"

"Because you've learned to distrust early in life. In a sense, you're like me. Perhaps before I leave, if everything goes well, I'll give you a copy. Seeing yourself through a lens is an experience most don't cherish until they can look back on those moments."

Banks took a deep breath. "When do we start?"

"Right now."

He squinted. "What that mean?"

"My cameramen are taping your family members as we speak." Whoyawanmetabe swallowed all of his liquor. "Shall we begin too?"

There were cameras everywhere, and although Whoyawanmetabe was not in the room, all were keenly aware that he was somewhere in the mansion posted up and watching. After all, this was his wish so why would he wait until after the cameras rolled to see the footage?

The mood was all off.

This was supposed to be dinner but with the cameras filming, the Lou's were determined to make it a music video. The first thing they did was come late dripped in gold chains and no shirts. And with the Wales and Nunez families

By T. STYLES

already seated and eating, they used them as cast members in their performance.

First on the scene was Mason, who held a bottle of champagne to his mouth. Since he'd come to the island he taxed Banks' bar so hard, it would be dry in a week.

This was certain.

Behind Mason were his sons Arlyndo, Howard, Patterson and Derrick who had gotten drunk earlier in the day. Jersey dragged in slowly behind them, embarrassed and concerned for whatever was about to happen due to a Louisville once again.

"Why ya'll sitting in here all stiff and shit!" Mason yelled, walking up to Banks as his sons flopped into positions on the right side of the table. "They want a show, lets give them a show."

Banks yanked Mason's wrist and pulled down to whisper in his ear. "Fuck is wrong with you? Huh? Why you tripping?"

Mason snatched away and dusted off his arm. As if his very touch soiled his ego.

"What? You wanted me to fall in line right, so this is me falling in line." He then walked up to one of the cameramen who stepped back to keep him in focus within his lens. "Did I tell ya'll how I got here? On Wales Island the first time?" Mason said to the cameras, all extra close and shit. "It really is an interesting story to be honest."

Silence.

"I sat in the storage area of Banks' plane," he burped a gaseous bubble of alcohol. It fogged up the lens. "Even stayed in his house the whole time without this nigga knowing." He looked at Banks as if he pitied him not. "I could've killed the nigga and yet, here he is still alive due to my grace. Back in the day he was king but man has he been—"

"Sit down, Mason," Banks said softly, although his anger had risen to levels not seen since his son was murdered. "You making a fool of yourself, your wife and your sons."

"We good over here," Howard said. "Worry about yourself, *Unc.*"

Banks glared at the fool.

"I ain't got a problem with my Pops either," Patterson said. "We good over here."

Derrick and Arlyndo chose to remain silent.

Besides, Arlyndo was too troubled about Minnie and Tobias.

Mason looked at Jersey who looked away in embarrassment. In response, the cameras moved in closer to catch her expression. There was no denying how she felt inside. It was literally written all over her face, by way of a wrinkled forehead and a lower gaze.

Knowing her for over twenty years, Mason read his wife's body reactions. "You know what, I'm not even surprised," Mason continued, drinking more liquor. "I've always been an embarrassment to my wife." He sat down in an available seat. "Why should now be any different?"

Jersey opened her mouth to respond, looked at the camera pointing her way and closed her mouth. Thinking it was best to remain silent.

Howard, on the other hand, grabbed a chair from one side of the table, picked it up and wedged it between Joey and Cassandra.

"Fuck is you doing, man?" Joey yelled shoving him with a closed fist on the forearm. "Back the fuck up and sit over there by your own people."

"Nigga, shut up," he responded breath as dank as a dumpster in a city alley.

"Can you please move?" Cassandra asked Howard calmly.

"Move for what?" He responded, "You work here don't you? Ain't you supposed to be servicing my needs? In the kitchen or something?"

Cassandra, distraught, ran out of the room. Joey glared at Howard and followed and of coursé a camera was close behind the duo.

As the Lou's continued to put on a show they were clearly enjoying, Banks grew incensed. It was all he could do to remain in place and strong for those he felt needed a firm presence. But there were so many questions and not enough answers. He was playing chess with a stranger and couldn't decipher his next move. Whoyawanmetabe had always been mysterious but even still he couldn't imagine what he really wanted.

And so, he remained seated and silent, studying everyone down to the cameramen, knowing that before long all would be revealed.

The next day, Banks and Mason sat in one of the guestrooms off the east end of the property. Their chairs were side by side even though it was obvious there was a lot of tension between them. Whoyawanmetabe sat across from them, facing both men while cameras were aimed at Banks and Mason...interview style.

It was showtime.

"So, where did you both meet?" Whoyawanmetabe asked.

Banks looked away. "I thought you were going to be following us. You ain't say nothing about interviews. So why we here?"

Amused in his question and anger, Mason grabbed the Hennessey bottle, took a swig and burped. "On the block. That's were we met."

Whoyawanmetabe smiled and formed his hands into a steeple. "Allow me to be more specific. Where on the block?"

Banks shifted in his seat as a warm heat rush coursed up his body, causing his face to redden. This was going to blow up, he was certain. "In Baltimore. Like I said a few days ago. We were friends. No different than any other young niggas growing up in the hood."

Mason looked at Banks and chuckled once. "We were way different."

Whoyawanmetabe nodded. "I need more, Mr. Wales."

Banks sighed. "What you mean?"

Whoyawanmetabe sat back in his chair. "Were you close?"

"As close as you can be as kids." Banks said doing his best to control the narrative. "I mean, we had a lot of growing up to do before a real friendship came along but we made it work. That's why we still cool now." He was lying and the room knew it.

They were anything but cool.

Mason laughed and took another sip.

"You want to say something?" Whoyawanmetabe asked him.

Still on joke time, Mason covered his mouth with a fist and spoke through the hole. "Nah. Not really. I'ma let him direct the show as usual."

"The sooner you both tell me the truth and I get what I need, the sooner I'll be gone." He leaned in, hands on both knees. "We can do this easy or slow. Your choice."

Mason faced Banks. "Banks and I were lovers and—"

"Mason!" Banks yelled, hoping to stop him where they sat.

"I know already, Banks," Whoyawanmetabe said. "Everybody in Baltimore does by now. There's no need in trying to hide."

"So that's what all this shits about?" Banks said through clenched teeth. "To expose my personal business? To expose my life?"

Whoyawanmetabe grinned. "All I'm saying is we all know."

"You see, he knows already." Mason grinned harder and ran his hand down his mouth before stopping at his chin. "She was my first bitch." He looked over at Banks as he leveled disrespectful insult after insult. "I mean, she was my girl since this shit being televised and all." He waved at the camera. "I fucked her and everything."

The world paused.

Banks was so heated his body swayed a little to the right. The level of anger he felt in the moment couldn't be measured. It was as if his body floated and he was certain of one thing, even if they survived this situation, their bond would be destroyed-destroyed.

Unable to continue with the interview, Banks rose and moved toward the exit.

"Mr. Wales, shall we tape your family instead?" Whoyawanmetabe said. "Since you are unwilling to continue? Maybe your wife? Or children?"

Banks turned around but slowly. His nostrils flared.

"I find that young people always do better with these types of things anyway. They think its like social media." He continued. "Now I'd prefer to get to know you more instead of them. Either way it's your call."

Upon hearing the threat, even Mason sobered up a little.

Banks ran both hands down his face, breathed into his palms and returned to his seat. He leveled a sinister glare at Whoyawanmetabe. "What you want to know?"

"Is what Mason said true? Were you two a couple?"

"You said you knew the story."

"Not the details, Mr. Wales. I'm here for the details."

Banks looked over at Mason and back at him. "Mason was something to do when I was a kid. I didn't take anything going on between us as genuine. Even then I had a girl but he couldn't understand. Couldn't let go. I basically used the nigga for money and pizza. But he always wanted more. I wouldn't be surprised if the same rings true today. He would drop to his knees right now if I let him."

Now it was Mason who grew enraged, while Whoyawanmetabe sat back and loved every bit of it. "So he looked into the relationship a little deeper than you wanted."

"That's exactly what I'm saying." Banks nodded. "He always has a way of pushing toward what doesn't want him. He the type of nigga who thinks you can push a square peg into a circle. And he'll always be that type. As I'm sure you can see by now."

Mason sat back, arms crossed tightly over his chest. He was assassinating his character with each blow.

Whoyawanmetabe smiled as if he'd just taken a hit of cocaine. "Well, we have enough for now." He rose. "Get used to this type of thing. And who knows, maybe it'll help you two work out whatever you have going on. Because by the looks of it, something is still there. Brewing under the surface."

Whoyawanmetabe left but one cameraman remained to cover whatever argument blew up after his exit. At this point the cameras were with them so much, that nobody gave a fuck anymore Besides, emotions were too high to conceal their feelings and so they unleashed no matter how many lenses sparkled their way.

"So you really used me when we was younger?"

"Fuck is wrong with you?" Banks growled, ignoring his question.

Mason smiled. "What you barking 'bout now?"

"Is this really a game for you? Do you really treat everything seriously in life like it's a joke?" Banks continued, jumping up from his seat.

"I always push to what I want?" He said sarcastically. "Remember?"

"Am I tripping or didn't you see that nigga snap the Nunez girl's neck? Were you—"

"Yeah, I saw it!" Mason leapt up from his chair. "Stop saying the same shit over and over."

"So fuck is you playing for?" Banks continued.

Mason walked a few feet away. "You asked me to participate in this shit, and I have a plan."

94                    By T. STYLES

Banks stepped back. This couldn't be happening. After all of his pleas for his oldest friend to fall the fuck back, he just couldn't bring himself to follow basic instructions. "Why are you like this?"

Silence.

"It's not enough for you to let shit play out, you still think you can control the situation even if it's not working."

"When you see what I have planned I want you to talk that shit then. Because it's going to be me who saves our families."

Banks approached him slowly. He wanted to appeal to that space in him that resonated with the *Mason and Blakeslee days.* When they were two kids, sitting on top of the steps in front of their building wanting it all.

Taking a deep breath he said, "Mason, please, I'm begging, if you ever gave a fuck about me or my family, please, man, don't do anything right now. The shit will backfire in your face, I promise you. Let shit play how it got to play for a minute. At least for a couple of days."

Mason looked at the camera and back at Banks. "I gotta do what I gotta do. And I'ma leave it at that."

# CHAPTER NINE

Like a young child doing a dance routine for attention, the sun did all it could to get Minnie, who sat below on the beach, to notice her extraordinary rays. But Minnie's heart was broken and not even the warmth of the sun's love could help.

Sitting yoga style on the sand, although she wanted things back to normal, where Harris was alive and well, she thanked God that at least for the moment she had her memories.

Despite the cameraman being near by, she was just about to take a nap, which meant he would have to follow someone else. Lately she enjoyed rest so much because when she was sleeping she didn't have to worry about the looming danger on the island.

Lying back, she was dozing off when Arlyndo walked up, wanting to talk. The one thing she was certain of after remembering how Arlyndo kidnapped her against her will was that their relationship had run its course. She also knew that telling him was not worth the trouble because she had other things to worry about.

"You know what I was thinking?" Arlyndo asked as he took a seat next to her flesh. He was as close as he could be without touching her, something she told him repeatedly she didn't want.

She took a deep breath, not up for conversation. "Arlyndo, please stop." She sat up.

"You remember me crawling into your window that night...That everything kicked off?"

Minnie burst out in laughter and her reaction shocked herself. It was at that moment that she realized that somewhere deep, she still had a place in her heart that belonged exclusively to him. "Do I remember?" She giggled. "You almost got me in trouble that night."

He shook his head as he recalled his life flashing before his eyes. "What the fuck was I thinking?"

"You asking me?" She said with a smile.

"I could've fucking broke my neck or something if I fell back trying to get into your bedroom window." He chuckled and shook his head softly. "I guess I would do anything for you though." His voice grew softer. "Even now. Even now." He repeated. "Minnie I would...I mean..." He moved closer and their skin merged until she pushed him back.

"Arlyndo, please don't."

"I'm serious! I'm so fucking serious," he yelled, slamming a fist to palm.

*There he go again.* She thought. *Losing his temper.*

"Minnie, I know you've been avoiding me, okay? I...I know you don't want me around and its ripping me up, baby. You hear me? It's ripping me up. Please don't do this to us. We been through too much. The rest should be easy."

"Not avoiding you."

"But you are though. I mean, will you hate me forever?" His voice resembled nails screeching down a chalkboard.

She turned her body to look into his eyes. Brushing sand off her toes she said, "I need you to understand something very serious. No place in my heart do I have your name and hate in the same area." She touched his hand. "No place, Arlyndo. I'm just; I'm just trying to get myself together. To, to be better for—"

"You sure you don't hate me though?" His mind was on one track and he couldn't receive her words. "Even after I tried to take you to Mexico when you didn't want to go? And you hurt your head because—"

"No place, Arlyndo." She repeated softly.

He nodded and looked at the beach. "Then what can I do? I mean, I...I know I try too hard sometimes. I know I push too much and I can't explain the feeling of, of, wanting somebody so badly that, that, you don't make the best moves. But how was I to know I would meet my first love so early? Please, Minnie, we grew up in love. We grew up in love so...so...so please don't tear us apart. I'll get on my knees if you want."

What could she say to make things better? To convince him they were done.

She smiled and looked downward, at the sand particles covering her big toe. "I think when we get past all of this maybe we can—"

"Don't say it."

"Arlyndo, you don't even know what I'm about to say."

"I do. Whenever you about to break my heart, your eyes lower. And you can't look at me." He grabbed her hand softly. "But I need you to believe in us. And I need you to look at me when you talk to me. See then if you can say the same things."

"Maybe I look down because whenever you wanna get serious, I gotta brace myself for impact."

"Impact?"

"You blow up, Arlyndo. Every time. And I love you but that shit be fucking up my mind." She caressed the side of his face and he trembled at her touch. "Just once I would like to be able to have grown folk conversation without fear of...of..."

His brows rose. "I would never hurt you."

"You sure about that?"

Silence.

"I'm willing to do whatever I have to," Arlyndo continued. "Just tell me what you want." He threw his hands up in the air. "Just say the words even if they hurt."

"Okay, if you're being honest, if you're being true, I think we need space. At least for a little while anyway."

This was not what he had planned.

Arlyndo got up and walked a few feet away, his back in her direction. Face on the ocean. "What that mean though? Be more specific."

"Arlyndo—"

"I just wanna know what that mean!" He yelled at the sea.

Her breath rose and fell inside her chest. "I don't know, I mean, I gotta figure some things out. Look at how much my life has changed. My brother is dead. We on an island and we got a man around right now circling us with cameras. At least give me a little space to figure my current situation out. That's all I'm asking."

Arlyndo looked back at the cameraman and sure enough, he had moved closer, something they always did when conflict rose. In fact, if the fighting got really juicy, all available cameramen on deck would go on scene at the same time, leaving the less conflicting situation alone.

Mason nodded. "I'll give you all the time you need."

"You sure about that?"

He sat next to her. "Yeah. I want you happy when we get back together."

"That means you can't bring the topic of 'us' up no more." She paused. "About us getting in a relationship or nothing."

"As long as you don't leave me, we can do that."

She smiled.

And then, from the corner of her eye, she saw Tobias submerge into the water. He was wearing black trunks and no shirt. Body on the ready. Every part of him was chiseled. For a moment she found her attention drawn to him like a magnet and unfortunately for all parties involved, Arlyndo noticed too.

"So this the reason you wanna back off?" He yelled jumping up.

She frowned and looked up at him. Realizing her error. Damn, why couldn't she look away? "What?"

"You want me to fall back while you fuck that nigga?" He pointed across the beach at him. "All on the island and shit?"

"Arlyndo, this is what I be talking about! What is wrong with you? Why you gotta be so raw-raw all the fucking time? Take a break! If nothing else for your health!"

"Bitch, shut the fuck up! I'm not about to sit on the sidelines while you build a whole 'nother situation with him!" He continued, pointing at Tobias who was unaware that an argument had brewed in his honor. "Where I gotta watch!"

"Then close your eyes."

"What, whore?" He yelled stomping up to her, sand clouds with each step.

"I can't with you no more." She leaned back and closed her eyes. "I'm done." She prayed he'd leave.

He didn't.

Arlyndo continued to pace in place, kicking up sand in the process. Letting his anger take the reigns, he rushed over to Tobias. The moment the man came up for air, he met the water again when Arlyndo struck him with a quick blow to the lower jaw.

Minnie and the cameraman went rushing to the scene. "Arlyndo stop!" She yelled, trying to grab him as he continued to pick Tobias up and hit him in the face.

"Nah, if you want this pretty boy, you gonna have him fucked up then!" Arlyndo moved to strike him again.

This time however, Tobias was able to block the blow and drop Arlyndo to the ocean. The brawl was grueling although the salt water wouldn't allow the severity of the fight to be shown, due to lapping at their bruised faces, washing blood away in the process.

# CHAPTER TEN

Cassandra was lying on her bed, crying about losing two sisters since meeting the Wales family. Her life before encountering the Americans wasn't the best, there was poverty, but at least they were *all* alive.

She recalled endless times where they would pick fresh fruit and make island dishes to eat them behind their decrepit home, on the other end of the island. Overlooking the ocean. With spices so sweet the taste lingered long after the meal was digested.

Although she, Emetine, Tobias and Roxana found a balanced serenity between poverty and the beauty of the island, her mother and other family members wanted more.

Always more.

And so they introduced themselves to Banks when he was building the fortress. When he was making plans for his family in paradise.

And now, after losing two members she loved, she wondered if it was all worth it. The only peace she got was that for some reason, the cameras didn't always venture to her side of the mansion, unless a Wales or Lou member was near.

With her pillow soaked, she was shocked when she rolled over only to see Joey walking through the door, a cameraman on his heels. "Joey, please leave me alone. I don't...I just need some peace." She spoke to him but her eyes were on the large camera hanging over the stranger's shoulder, which appeared eager to take a bit more of her serenity.

Wanting to spend some time alone with Cassandra, he took a deep breath and faced the unwanted person in the room. "Can you stay out here right quick?" He asked the cameraman. "I just wanna see how she's doing that's all. I promise I'll open the door after I'm done."

The man's face appeared to be replaced with a huge lens as he spoke from behind the device. "You know the rules." He adjusted a little so that the camera could sit more comfortably on his shoulder. "Everything but sex and sleep can be filmed. If you got a problem with it, talk to Whoyawanmetabe."

Joey sighed and entered as the cameraman walked in also, holding up the corner of the room, away from the couple. He called himself giving a little privacy to the duo. But it wasn't because he cared about giving them space. His reason was strategic. He was quite aware that the farther away he was, the more easily they would possibly forget that he was there, allowing for a better exchange for his taping.

Joey looked at him and back at Cassandra. "How...how are you doing? I mean, can I like get you anything? Anything at all?"

She looked at the camera and back at him. Irritated above all. "You know how I am, Joey. I mean, you tell me, how would you feel if both of your sisters were murdered in less than six months?" She tugged at the white t-shirt she wore, which showed the curves of her full breasts. "But don't waste my time. What do you want?" She wiped her hair over her shoulder and it dripped over her right breast.

He sighed. "Can I...sit down?" He pointed at the bed.

She shrugged. "Whatever, this your house not mine."

Big facts.

"I know you're mad at me." He positioned his body to be able to look into her eyes. "And—"

"Mad at you for which part?" She interrupted, her cream face reddening. "Fucking my sister or getting me pregnant and not caring?"

"Cassandra, it's not that I didn't care. It was more that I didn't know. I mean, you talked about getting pregnant by me when my father was gone but you didn't tell me that you were actually knocked up. I would've stepped up if I knew but—"

"I'm not crying because of you, Joey. I'm crying because, because—" She looked at the cameraman and back at him. If only he would leave she could be more forthcoming. "Because I don't understand it all. And I'm afraid my family is disposable and not yours. Why else would Whoyawanmetabe hurt a member of my family and not one of the members who disrespected him?"

He glared and held a large breath in his lungs before releasing. "So...so you want me to be hurt instead? And my family to be dead?"

Her head hung like a wilting rose. "That's not what I'm saying."

He touched her arm. "Listen, I wanted to tell you, I mean, I never got the chance to say that

I'm sorry for, for hurting you. For not being there when you needed me. My pops was gone and, and I didn't know how to act. Started tripping and fucking everything because..." He shrugged. "I don't know, you and your sister are so beautiful that...I guess I lost my mind." He dragged a hand down his face. "And I'm not making any excuses. It's my bag and I accept it fully. I just want you to know that I'm here now. Available if you need me." He held her hand.

She sniffled. "Wow."

"What?"

"I didn't think I'd hear those words. I mean, so much time has passed and, and I started to believe you never cared about killing our baby."

He removed his hand. "Killing our baby?" His neck craned backward. "How was that on me?"

She glared. "Are you serious? I had to sit by and watch you do the ultimate. You know how it felt to see you fucking my sister and—"

"Hold up!" He interrupted. "When I apologized, it was for hurting you by sleeping with Emetine. But it wasn't because I take the blame for killing our baby. I mean, I don't know if your body couldn't hold it or—"

"Get out, Joey," she yelled as the camera moved in greedily, wanting to get each moment. She was not about to hear him insult her ability to have children. "Please."

"But I'm talking to you though."

"Well I don't have anything else to say," she continued, standing up, whipping the hair off her shoulder.

He looked down at his hands and took a deep breath. "I think we got off on the wrong—"

"You know what, if you not going to leave, I'll go." She stormed out of the room, feet slapping down the marble.

He leapt up. "Cassandra!"

She moved so quickly down the hall and out of the Nunez house that the cameraman couldn't keep up. Before long she was in the Wales mansion and unfortunately she banged right into Howard and Patterson Louisville who were exiting the bowling alley.

They were trouble personified.

When they saw her she was as sweet as honeyed milk.

"Damn," Patterson said looking over her body as he greedily rubbed his hands together. Her nipples were hardened due to the wind slapping against her skin as she ran, making herself look more edible in the moment. "I been trying to find out where your fine ass been around here from the moment we landed." He ran his fingers down her arm and grabbed her warm hand, squeezing it inside his clammy palm.

"Just leave me alone," she said snatching away from him. She tried to walk around his frame, and out of harm's way, but Patterson jumped in her face. "Please, I, I have a lot on my mind right now."

"Well let me help get you right then." Patterson said sinisterly.

"If you let her get away you weak," Howard said, biting his bottom lip. He wanted to see violence so bad his veins throbbed.

"Like I said, I have to go," she continued. She looked back hoping someone else saw what was about to occur. They didn't. It was just them three. Her breath warmed her whole body making her dizzy. She was in danger and she knew it.

Suddenly the cameraman following her didn't seem like such a bad idea.

Except he was nowhere to be found.

Because she ran away.

"What if I don't want you to leave?" Patterson continued, as they stepped in front of her. They both meant her ill will, but it was Patterson who touched her face, gritty fingertips running along the side of her cheek. "I figured we could have a little fun and—"

She smacked his hand off her waist. "Don't touch me!"

He laughed, and stepped to the side, as if she'd won. The moment her foot made a move in the opposite direction, he snatched her by the waist and dragged her into the bowling alley like a disobedient child. A hand slammed over her mouth to silence her pleas.

With her in his possession like a bag full of stolen money, he closed the door behind himself.

Howard, with a smirk on his face, held up the front door while his brother did his thing. His body pressing against the cool door as his mind imagined everything he was possibly doing to her on the other side.

You see, Howard got off on the rough parts of humanity.

Besides, he had seen his father, Mason, abuse his mother all of his life, and felt like it was best to take what you want. Like father like son.

Two minutes later, Spacey walked up to the bowling alley preparing to play. "Why you blocking the door?"

Howard sat up straight and looked him up and down once. "The lanes are closed." He licked his lips. "Why you here?"

Spacey frowned. "Ain't nobody say nothing about the lanes being closed."

Howard glared and stepped up closer. "You calling me a liar?"

"Get out my face." Spacey moved to walk around him and into the alley when Howard shoved him back with a palm to the lower neck.

"Fuck is your problem. I said beat it, roach."

"Stop!"

"Listen, I get it," Howard started, grabbing his own crotch. "You think because you been away that I still won't make you suck my dick?" He lowered his head and squinted his eyes to look directly into his face. "Don't get it twisted, time won't stop you from dropping on them knees if I make you." He gripped his dick in his jeans.

Spacey's heart thumped.

Although time had passed, Howard making him perform oral sex on him, since he could remember, never left his mind. In fact, it haunted him in ways he never imagined. By destroying his bond with women. By making him believe that perhaps he did something to warrant such attentions from a man he once considered family. In the end he questioned his manhood, his masculinity and his life.

Feeling embarrassed, Spacey said, "Whatever, man. Do what you want." He turned to walk away when suddenly he heard a female scream. Slowly Spacey turned back around and faced the door.

He had to do something.

Right?

"Keep walking," Howard said rubbing the skin of his neck before crossing his arms across his chest tightly, causing his muscles to bubble.

"What's, what's going on in there?"

Howard glared. "You must be a glutton for punishment. Didn't I tell you to get the fuck on up the hallway?"

"I said who's, who's in there?" He stuttered. Suddenly his mind went to the worse case situation. "Is it Minnie? Or Shay? Maybe my mother?"

"What?" Howard glared as if disgusted. "Nah, man. Patterson just—"

Suddenly a cameraman came down the hallway eager to get the shot. Spacey used his presence as a diversion tactic. With wide eyes, Spacey yanked the door open just as Cassandra came running out with her clothes falling off her half naked body. The cameramen ran behind her, as Patterson walked out, with his zipper down.

"What, what you do to her?" Spacey asked Patterson.

"Scram, clown," Patterson said walking slowly in the opposite direction, away from surveillance.

Spacey stood by the door with his jaw hung open. He knew Howard was a monster and that Mason was too. But was it possible that every member in the Louisville family was a savage?

Did the bloodline automatically mean tainted?

"I know you think you know what happened in there," Howard continued. "But if I were you, I wouldn't say shit about this day. Make it a memory. Unless you want the same thing to happen to you too." He winked and walked away.

# CHAPTER ELEVEN

It was midnight and all of the cameramen were asleep as Banks left his marital bedroom and strolled down the corridors of the mansion. Lately this was his best and favorite time walking through his home, to avoid the cameras. Although isolation never worked perfectly, because the cameramen would still invade his privacy, Banks still preferred being secluded because it gave him time to plan his attack silently.

Without the scrutinizing eyes of his wife watching his every move. Without the look of confusion from his children bearing down on him. Without the Nunez family's murmurs where they hated the day he picked them to care for his home and more importantly, when they returned, only to learn a madman had taken over.

Nah, he needed this time above all to get his thought process together.

When he walked toward his kitchen, he was surprised to hear whispering, believing the cameramen and Whoyawanmetabe to be asleep.

No one was usually up this time of night except him. Besides, everyone was a nervous wreck since Whoyawanmetabe and his cameramen consumed every part of their lives and so sleep became a close friend.

So who was awake now?

When he bent the corner, he was stunned to see the most unlikely of duos together. It was Mason and Rosa Nunez. They were standing by a counter, their backs now in his direction, within the darkness. Only the moonlight shone against their faces.

Banks squinted. "What's, what's going on?"

It startled both of them and Rosa quickly separated from Mason. Her expression guilty and full of secrets. There was also something on the counter out of Banks' view.

"Nothing," Mason spoke first, hiding the item. "Them cameramen keep eating our food and shit. So we were grabbing something to eat."

"Yeah...uh...Bet told me about that. I'll talk to—"

"Don't bother," Mason interrupted. "It won't change a thing." He sighed. "What you, what you doing up though?"

Banks walked slowly toward the counter, pushed him softly away and looked at a pitcher of sangria. An open coconut sat next to it, which had been pricked and cut several times.

Frowning Banks asked them, "What is this? Because I know neither one of you took to the night *just* to make fucking punch."

Mason looked over Banks shoulder at the doorway, walked out into the hallway and quickly came back. It was as if the brisk bop stuffed him with enough energy to go off. "It's a fucking plan! That's what it is!"

Banks scratched his temple. "What you mean a plan? How is juice—"

"We have been going about things the wrong way," Mason interrupted in a violent whisper. "When the man practically told us *how* to get rid of him. So I figure if we make this shit, and he drinks it, we be free."

"Are you, are you saying—"

"It will be quick, Mr. Wales." Rosa said softly, her accent thick with worry. "And in return, my daughter, my precious daughter would have the justice she deserves. What is wrong with that?"

Banks touched Rosa on her shoulder before running a warm hand down her face. He knew first hand how it felt to lose a child and in the rumble around the mansion he never got a chance to tell her that he was apologetic. He never got a chance to console her so that she knew she wasn't alone. "I'm so sorry, Rosa. I truly am. For Emetine. For Oswalda."

She looked down and more tears rolled like raindrops on a car window.

"Neither of the girls will die in vain, but you have to trust me. This is not the way." He paused. "Now, please, leave us alone for a second. I want to talk to Mason in private."

"Si'." She nodded and walked toward the door. Before exiting she turned around and said, "Don't drink the sangria. It's already tainted." She exited with the wind.

Banks dragged two hands down his face before clenching them tightly in front of Mason. It took everything in him to prevent 'the laying on of hands'.

"What you doing? I can't believe after everything you still with the dumb shit. When you know what it could cost us. I mean, what's wrong with you? You on coke?"

"What, nigga? I got shit I gotta do for me and my people, man," Mason shrugged. "Plans I wanna make work so that means getting back to Maryland. And the last thing I need is this Jamaican taking up all my time by putting me on a reality TV show like I'm some sort of bitch. This plan will work. Me and Rosa laid it all out. I'm surprised you didn't use her before. She knows how to make poisons and all that other voodoo type shit." He chuckled quietly. "Relax, Banks. I got this. I got us."

Banks walked away, his back in Mason's direction. "If you do this it'll be a big mistake. Do you hear what I'm saying? I don't know why but I feel it in my heart. Please, put the pause on all this until I can sort stuff out in my head. And I know my process slow but I'm thinking. I swear to God I am."

"So why not fly us out right now? So we can go back home. Grab the keys or something."

"Planes don't use keys," Banks corrected him. "And they have a man sleeping on my plane and Whoyawanmetabe's plane too. They doing shifts and everything."

"I get it," Mason said pointing at him. "You just mad because you ain't the one who thought of this poison shit first." He smiled pointing at the sangria. "Don't worry, I'll let you keep the credit, just as long as you—"

"Mason, please, don't do this." Banks continued to beg like a repeated recorder, walking up to him. "You gonna fuck up what I got brewing."

"You mean one of your slow ass plans?" He paused. "Nigga, my kids in this house now. My wife is in this house. I'm sorry, but I can't trust your instincts. The cost is too heavy."

"Mason, this dude is not like one of the hood niggas you know on the corner. It won't be that easy to get at him. But since your mind is already made up, you'll see." Banks shook his head and walked away.

# CHAPTER TWELVE

*T*he cold air was making it known that the warm days were about to be a thing of the past, before old man Winter came through in all his vengeance. But for now, keeping court outside was still possible without suffering severe freezer burn while Mason stood behind Blakeslee in front of the school, as she trembled with fear.

*She was waiting.*

*To try again.*

*The school bell rang a few minutes earlier and Nikki hadn't exited with the throng of children who were already in the schoolyard and Blakeslee was losing nerve.*

*Could she tell her what was on her mind, without facing additional rejection? Rejection that stung so hard it caused her chest to literally hurt? Was she built like that?*

*"I don't know about this,"* Blakeslee said looking back at Mason who always appeared to hang over her shoulder. Watching it all. *"What if, what if she—"*

"Don't worry about..." Mason squinted and looked across the way at the kids piling out. Sometimes he found pleasure in Blakeslee's misery although he wasn't old enough to understand why. "There she go right there," he pointed a stiff finger toward the crowd.

Blakeslee followed his gaze and saw Nikki walking out of the schoolyard wearing a red leather jacket. It was new and Blakeslee shivered because she was quite aware that Hector purchased it for her, throwing his money around like falling leaves.

"She so pretty," Blakeslee said, allowing a cool puff cloud of fog to roll from her lips. "One day when I get enough money I'ma take care of her better. Like get a Mercedes for her and everything."

Mason looked at Blakeslee, careful to examine each part of her face. The soft way her braids unraveled from the rows around her hair. The way her yellow skin reddened the moment the cold air whipped at her cheeks.

"She not prettier than you though," Mason whispered.

"Huh?" Blakeslee responded. She was so focused on Nikki that she didn't hear a word he uttered.

124  By T. STYLES

"Nothing." How he wished he could tell her what he felt but he was learning that when it came to Nikki, Blakeslee had laser focus and could be mean as a rattlesnake if someone got in the way. Infringing on her love for Nikki would be bad for business.

He had to back all the way up.

Blakeslee continued to watch Nikki from afar and smiled. She seemed graceful as she moved but more than anything, she was alone. Quickly Blakeslee headed toward her, smiling with hope big enough to fill the space that surrounded Baltimore.

"I'm going with you." Mason said.

She paused. "If Hector sees you with me he'll get mad that we still friends," she looked at him and back at her. "Maybe you should just leave me alone, Mason. To talk to her. That way I can see where she coming from first."

The fear of being isolated again by Blakeslee, because of Nikki, stung him like a wasp. He'd been a part of the trio before, only to be cut out like gangrene and he didn't want that to happen again. He needed to be a part of Blakeslee's world, above all else. "That's the thing," Mason moved closer, grabbing her hand. "I want to tell you something about him first."

She readjusted her stance, as if bracing for the worst. Slowly she turned her body around to face him completely. Her brown eyes resting on him in fear, screaming please don't hurt my feelings with terrible news. "What about...what about Hector?"

Mason moved closer, as if he was about to drop something so heavy he needed her hands to help hold it. "I never finish telling you what happened that night. At my party he finger fucked this girl." He tapped her shoulder with the back of his hand. "And, and get this, I think they had sex too."

Her eyes widened. "You lying. I mean, why you ain't tell me before?"

"I promise you I'm not lying. And I'm telling you now." He shrugged. "You can ask him yourself if you don't believe me."

Now the bearer of bad news, Blakeslee rushed over to Nikki and ripped everything she learned about Hector in one breath. The finger fuck. The sex. The pride she felt about revealing the truth diminished when she saw Nikki's panged face.

Hector, who just exited the building, approached his crying girlfriend at the wrong damn time.

By T. STYLES

Mason slid closer to the group also.

Embarrassed to have a crowd, Nikki yanked Hector's hand and walked a few feet away from the duo. "Did you, you go to Mason's party and...and...did you go?"

Hector shuffled a little, and stuffed his hands into his coat pockets. "Yeah, why, what he, what he, what he...say?" He looked over at Mason who grinned. "'Cause don't forget people be trying to break us up. Don't let—"

Nikki moved closer, fully prepared to claw at his face. "Did you finger fuck some girl?"

His eyes widened. "I mean, she was a freak and—,"

"I hate you!" Nikki stumbled backwards as tears rolled down her cheeks. "You promised you would never hurt me and you lied!"

He grabbed her elbow but she pounded at his chest with both fists. "But she ain't mean nothing to me. I don't even remember her name. I—"

That was worse.

At least a girl worth losing her for made things easier.

"I don't care! You embarrassed me in front of my friends too." She huffed and puffed. "I will never forgive you."

"Nikki, please!" He put an arm around her waist.

"Fuck off me!" She slapped his hand off and stormed up to Blakeslee and Mason. Sniffling and wiping the tears away she said. "Ya'll walk me home."

"Sure," Blakeslee responded, as if she was wearing a cape.

"We got you," Mason added. "Don't worry about shit."

An hour later Blakeslee and Nikki were sitting on the stoop of their building. Nikki was still heart broken but her mood had lightened, allowing her to remember why she and Blakeslee were so close. Time flew by as the girls talked about their lives and it was as if they didn't skip a beat. As if Blakeslee's deceased mother hadn't dragged her *out of Blakeslee's room, the night she learned they kissed.*

*They were as good together as the sun was to the sky.*

*The moon to the stars.*

*The sand to the sea.*

*All natural was their bond.*

"...so her entire butt was out in class, Blakeslee," Nikki said as she bumped her knee against hers as she laughed heartily. It didn't matter that the cold from the concrete burned like fire on their butts. They were together once again. "I don't know why the jeans split but it was crazy. Like, everybody was looking at it and we were like, are we really seeing her ass?"

"She may have wanted it out," Blakeslee continued. "I mean you say she a freak and stuff." They laughed lightly before things got quiet. It was a weird silence of things needing to be said although the energy was too tense to accept.

Blakeslee took the leap anyway.

"Nikki, I'm sorry about, you know...what my mother did to you. I know it hurt your feelings, I do. And I wish...like I wish I could take that back. And I'm sorry about Hector too."

She sighed deeply, as if trying to blow the pain she felt away. To the forgotten place that held the past like bones in a graveyard. "It's not your fault. I mean, he...he was wrong. He shouldn't even have been there."

"I know, but it's still not right. He should've treated you better than that. He should have loved you like—"

"What he doing over here?" Nikki asked, interrupting the conversation.

When Blakeslee looked across the way, toward the end of the fence leading to the street, she saw Hector creeping like a rat preparing to steal food.

"Just ignore him, Nikki." Her heart raced. She could feel his wanting to separate them again like a plucked grape from its vine. "All he gonna do is lie to you, right? You know that." She grabbed her hand demanding that she stay.

Slowly she peeled away, her eyes on him as fixed as a flashlight's shine. "Nah, I wanna hear what lies he about to pop off this time." Without another word, she quickly ran over to Hector and when their eyes met, it was obvious that suddenly she wasn't angry anymore.

Where was the rage?

*Where was the pain she so easily expressed earlier?*

*Why hadn't she kept the same energy?*

*Blakeslee was helpless and all she could do was watch her take him back again.*

*From afar she saw Hector speaking passionately, arms throwing up like branches in a storm. Mouth contorted as he expressed himself with the enthusiasm of a lost lover. His rage didn't appear to be directed toward her, although if he threw his hands any more forcefully, Nikki could've gotten hurt.*

*After what seemed like forever, although it was only two minutes, suddenly Nikki turned around and walked back toward Blakeslee, as Hector remained at the far end of the fence.*

*Waiting.*

*Watching.*

*Smiling.*

*But why?*

*When she approached Blakeslee, her anger seemed to be geared toward her all of a sudden. Like Blakeslee was the one who broke her heart when all she wanted was to protect Nikki and make sure she was safe. "Is it...is it true, Blakeslee?"*

*Silence.*

*"Blakeslee, is it true or not?" She yelled.*

*She rose and walked down the steps so that they were eye to eye. "I don't, I don't know what you—"*

*"Did you set Hector up or not? To be with that nasty girl at Mason's party?"*

*Blakeslee swallowed the lump forming in her throat as she realized she was set back once again. Of course she didn't know what Mason planned. He did the worst always on his own. Still, when she went over the plans with Mason, she didn't consider the blowback and now it was too late.*

*"I...I...didn't know he would do that thing with the other girls. I didn't know he would, he would hurt you like that. I—"*

*SMACK!*

*It took a few seconds but when Blakeslee finally realized she had been hit, Nikki had already returned arm and arm with Hector as they both walked away, taking Blakeslee's heart with them in the process.*

*He won, but it didn't stop Hector from turning back momentarily just to smile. Just to throw in her face that Nikki and he were supposed to be together, as God intended.*

*Blakeslee was sick to the stomach.*

*When she considered Mason's plan, she didn't know it would push her further back from her goal.*

*Further back from Nikki.*

*And for the moment, she wondered, what other trouble Mason would get her into in life. It would be years later before she got that answer.*

Shay and Derrick Louisville had just left Minnie and Tobias who were eating sandwiches in the Nunez's kitchen. After getting shot not to long ago and having his big toe cut off by Banks in rage, Derrick chose to spend the time on the island with Shay who needed his full attention due to losing Harris.

Now alone with Tobias, Minnie did her best not to look at his badly bruised face due to being knocked out by Whoyawanmetabe's goon and the fight from Arlyndo on the beach. But it was tough pretending not to see the scars.

Minnie looked over her shoulder at the door.

"Don't worry, the cameramen don't come here."

She smiled.

"Oh wait, you're not worried about the cameramen." He shook his head slowly. "You're worried about *him* aren't you? Arlyndo?"

Silence.

Tobias took a deep breath. "So you never told me how it tasted," he continued, watching her eat with a huge smile on her face. "Shay and Derrick seemed to like my food but you...I don't know."

A few bites fell from the corners of her mouth and he smiled as she tucked them back inside.

He had gotten his answer.

"Excuse me." She giggled. "It's, it's delicious. Sweet and spicy." She swallowed and took another bite. "What is it again?"

"It's a turkey peccadillo sandwich. A favorite in my family for generations." He placed his sandwich down, wiped his hands together and sat back. "Has raisins, garlic...I mean, a bit of everything to be honest."

"Well, thanks for making this for me...for us."
She put the last bite down. "I'm stuffed."

"Derrick and Shay...they've been together long?" He leaned closer. "I always see them on the beach, away from everybody else. I think they're on to something. To throw the cameras off."

"No, she's the daughter of my father's friend. Technically she's...like our sister and Derrick is Mason's son."

"He doesn't seem like them...the Lou's."

She nodded, trying not to think of Arlyndo who was the worst of them all. "He isn't. Doesn't like trouble."

"So, tell me why you decided to let me cook for you again, Ms. Minnesota."

She took a deep breath. "Guilt."

"What happened between me and Arlyndo wasn't your fault," he paused. "I keep explaining it to you. Hopefully soon you'll understand."

"I know, it's just that, Arlyndo is, he's...harsh at times." She smoothed her hair back even though it was tightly bound in a ponytail, with not a strand out of place. "He can't control his temper. And the saddest part, the thing that keeps bothering me is I think he really tries."

"I don't get it." He raked his fingers through his coal black hair. It seemed to shine more when he did, and Minnie noticed it all. To say the man was perfect was an understatement. "Why protect him like you do?"

She averted her eyes away from his beauty and looked down at what was left of her sandwich. "I don't protect him. But he connects his life with mine and I'm afraid if he doesn't get what he wants from me, he'll, he'll hurt me instead."

Tobias glared and sat up to the table. Two hands clutched together in an angry prayer. "Not while I'm here." He pointed at the table. A stiff finger that could've stabbed through the wood if he poked any harder.

She shrugged.

He touched her hand. "I'm serious. I will never let him hurt you."

"No, please don't say that," she pulled her hand away. "I realize it's in your nature to protect but I don't want that for myself anymore. A lot has happened over the past year because of me and I'm trying to be...different. It's time for me to own up to my shit and defend myself without getting others involved. I hope you understand."

He sat back and crossed his arms over his chest. He didn't want her going at Arlyndo alone but he had to respect her wishes. It made him feel her even more.

"Does Banks know how much Arlyndo's overpossesiveness has taken control of your life? How afraid you are?"

"No. If I tell him he'll react and he has so much more to worry about." She looked around the small Latin style kitchen. "It's beautiful here, but the fact we came early, to the island, was my fault. Me and Arlyndo's. Had I not told my father's secret at dinner one night, none of this would've happened."

"But then I wouldn't have met you."

Big facts.

She smiled.

He winked.

"But look," she cleared her throat and smoothed her neat ponytail backwards again. "I enjoyed the meal and I really am sorry but I must go." She stood up and rushed out a side door leading into the courtyard before he could dispute.

Although she didn't know why, for some reason she felt creeped out.

The moment she bent the corner heading to the big house, she ran into Arlyndo who was glaring her way.

"You whore," he said with all the rage he could muster. His teeth were clamped together so hard they could've turned to sand. "I always knew that about you, but after seeing you smiling in that nigga's face in the window, now it's clear."

He was a Peeping Tom by nature.

"Whatever," she said, attempting to walk around him, before his rigid body blocked further motion.

Arlyndo yanked her arm. "You won."

She snatched away, but not without his nails dragging a thin layer of skin, leaving blood tracks. "What you talking about now?" She attempted to rub the pain away.

"I won't chase you. I won't call you. I won't even tell you how much I love you." He moved closer. "But hear this, because this is when it gets good. I won't allow you to be with another nigga, not now, not ever."

"I'm not tripping off of—"

"Not Tobias." He continued cutting her off. "Not some city nigga. Not a college type dude either. Nobody. Because when you get into a relationship, and when you're happy and think shit's sweet, I will pull up on both of you when you least expect it and snap your fucking necks." His breath was heavy and rabid like a dog. Even down to the long lines of spit trailing the sides of his mouth.

"Arlyndo..." Her eyes were wide with fear. Where the fuck was the cameras when you needed them? "Look at you. You, you look crazy."

"You will never be happy, whore," he said softly. "I should've left you in the ditch I found you in. But if something happens in the future, I won't make that mistake again." He spit at her feet, globs of saliva weighing on her big toe.

Before storming away.

A soft glow from the lighting along the perimeter of the dining room tried to provide for an elegant evening, but tension was in the air. Everyone was seated at the dining room table and extensions had been added so there was room for all.

Oh joy!

Whoyawanmetabe sat at the far end. Banks on the other. On the right were the Wales family and on the left were the Louisville's along with the Nunez family. All were present except Rosa and Ives who went to get the drinks as the table was already filled with Latin dishes for the evening. Baited breath kept the guests company and within a few minutes she and her husband entered holding icy pitchers of coconut sangria.

This was the moment Banks dreaded.

His heart rate kicked up a notch as the ice cubes banged along the inside of the glass pitchers. It was obvious that Mason's plan, which Banks tried to veto many times, was underway.

Mason was so dead set on seeing the farce through, that he and Rosa had taken to hiding in corners, away from the cameras, to hash out the details. All Banks could do was warn his family not to drink the punch, no matter what.

"Sangria," Whoyawanmetabe smiled as he looked at the condensation forming along the pitchers. "This is a treat."

"Yeah, we wanted you to have something from your hometown." Mason said. "Rosa thought it would be complimentary with the meal."

"Complimentary huh?" Whoyawanmetabe said sarcastically.

Rosa nodded and smiled. It was the kind of smile that sat on a face of someone who was afraid to die, but had to be nice because it was the best thing to do to hide her ruse.

Slowly, Rosa filled everyone's glass except for Whoyawanmetabe's, hers and Ives's. When the drinks were gone, slowly she trailed over to Ives, removed the pitcher from his hand and poured Whoyawanmetabe's glass, followed by hers and Ives.

When all glasses were brimming with the drink, Rosa and Ives took their seats. Everyone was so afraid to move it was hard to breathe in the room. Almost as if someone had turned the heat up high, although the air was quite cool.

With everyone in place, Whoyawanmetabe clapped his hands together. "Okay, everybody raise your drinks in the air. We have so much to celebrate and I'm confident that my film, which you have all agreed to be a part of, will be everything I envisioned and more. I don't consider myself a director but I try."

Everyone cautiously raised their glasses in the air.

"I also want to say that I know the past few days have been rough. But we are almost at the finish line. Let us drink!"

With that, he drank the entire glass while everyone else sat theirs down. The moment the ice cubes brushed against his lips and Whoyawanmetabe burped, Mason grinned proudly. His sons, with the exception of Derrick, also found great amusement in the man falling victim so easily to his plan. All had been made aware he would die today. Secretly they hoped he'd be a better opponent.

But it was okay if he wasn't.

After all, Mason's plan had been successful. Whoyawanmetabe drank the poisonous juice that was poured into his glass and in a moment he would be dead, and the real celebration could begin.

This should be perfect.

Besides, Mason had thought of every area of his scheme. The drink from the pitcher that Ives held had the special weapon while the sangria in the other pitcher was edible and ready. Mason and Rosa even had a plan for the cameramen. All of his sons held knives under the table which they would use to cut their throats the moment Whoyawanmetabe dropped. Even the hidden pilot would fall prey once the door came crashing down that protected him.

Realizing he won, Mason sat back cockily in his chair as he tore into his meal. With Whoyawanmetabe's eminent death being near, his appetite suddenly returned. And his sons seemed in the mood to eat also as they tore into their food like savage beasts.

"You should've left," Mason told Whoyawanmetabe arrogantly. "Now it's too late." He continued, with his mouth full of food.

"Come again?" Whoyawanmetabe said calmly, biting into a beef empanada before dabbing the corners of his mouth with a linen napkin.

Banks fell back in his seat in frustration as he watched the scene unfold. Whether the plan worked or not, he felt Mason was way off in how he was going about the matter in regards to his attitude. Nothing about him was humble which always led to more strife.

For Banks.

"We begged you to leave this island but you didn't listen." Mason shrugged. "You thought it was a game but it's not. And now, you'll see." He dug into the bowl of Spanish rice with his fingers while dropping it into his mouth.

"Yep," Arlyndo added biting into his chicken before downing half the sangria in his cup. "You thought we were gonna just sit back and watch you do your thing?" He paused. "Is that it?"

"Stop starting trouble," Tobias said to Arlyndo.

"Nigga, don't say shit to me."

"I said I'm Latino!"

Minnie touched Tobias' hand, begging him not to further bait her ex-boyfriend. When Arlyndo saw their interaction he drank the rest of his sangria and promised to himself to murder Tobias before the night's end.

"You're doing a lot of grandstanding," Whoyawanmetabe said to Mason. "And your son too. You should be careful about such cockiness though. It may not serve you well."

"Nigga, fuck you." Mason said. "You're as good as dead."

Whoyawanmetabe's men moved closer to the table until he threw his hand up for them to pause. The Louisville clan thought the situation was funny and laughed heartily knowing that in a moment, when Whoyawanmetabe died, every cameraman would be swimming in his own blood.

Gashes to the necks or thrashes to the guts.

"You talk a lot," Whoyawanmetabe said to Mason. "Is it because you enjoy the sound of your own voice?"

Mason smiled and wiped the corners of his mouth. "Call it what you—"

Suddenly Arlyndo rose up and grabbed at his neck as if he were trying to drag a turtleneck down due to being too tight. In his wild agitation, the chair fell on the floor. His eyes bulged and he was pleading silently for help.

Confused, Mason and his family rushed to his aide with Banks right alongside them.

"What's wrong, son?" Mason begged as Arlyndo hit the floor. "Are you choking or something? Tell me what to—"

Arlyndo's skin slowly went from brown to blue before his eyes.

Mason felt faint but he tried to remain standing. He had zero skills in CPR and was totally useless. It was Banks who dropped to his knees and bent Arlyndo's neck as he used his finger to fish inside his mouth for what had choked him.

Banks was about his business, trying to save the kid who he referred to as nephew in life. He was so diligent that it was Banks' face that Arlyndo would cling to as he slipped into the afterlife.

Mason was another story altogether. The world appeared to spin as all became obvious. Someone had switched the punch and as a result, he lost his youngest child.

In a most ferocious way.

# CHAPTER THIRTEEN

It was a devastating time for all on Wales Island.

Shay traipsed over to Derrick who was sitting in the living room of the mansion with a dazed look on his face. He stared at the wall, as if replaying the scene of losing Arlyndo over and over. Although death was always a possibility in the Lou family, as it was in any family, it hit different somehow. In Derrick's mind it was clear that before now, he thought they were all invincible.

He was wrong.

"Derrick," she said softly, while standing a few feet before him, fiddling her fingers. "Derrick."

Her soft voice startled him to the present, where again he had to deal with his kid brother being gone. "Y...yeah."

"Is there anything I can do?" She asked softly.

He rolled his eyes up from her cute toes all the way to her doe like eyes. "No...I really wanna be left alone. Don't feel much like talking."

"I understand, I can sit with you in silence if you—"

"Fuck you want from me?" He yelled, jumping up from his seat before rushing toward her with fury. "It ain't like you give a fuck about me! You a Wales nigga right? And Wales niggas don't care about nobody but they self."

Shay's body trembled.

Up until that moment she assumed he was unlike his brothers and Mason. Void of anger. And now she was faced with understanding that he came from their same bloodline, which made him just as undomesticated. Filled with the same rage.

He didn't care that she was crying as he laid into her. She had hoped that he would help get her mind off of Harris on the island but that wasn't the case. "I'm sorry," she sobbed. "I—"

"Shay," Banks said softly entering the room. When she turned around she saw him and his entire family. "Are you okay?"

Derrick backed away from her, swallowed and walked quickly toward the exit. He was stopped with Banks' warm hand on his shoulder. "Son, I'm really sorry about Arlyndo."

Derrick looked at his hand and remembered when he cut his big toe. "Get ya' hands off me, dyke bitch." He yelled, storming out.

Banks took a deep breath as his family piled inside the living room, taking available seats on the couch. Although he hated his gender being thrown in his face, especially if it was wrong, he would allow him the slight for the moment. But if disrespect of any kind came in the days ahead, he would be forced to check him swiftly.

Moving over to Shay he said, "You can't be with him. You know that right?"

She nodded and took her seat next to Minnie, who held her closely; for they both had fallen for Lou men.

Banks took a deep breath and looked at his sons, daughter, Shay and Bet. "We have to be careful over the next few days." A cameraman entered the room and Banks stared him down with the intensity of a man preparing to break the rules if he didn't leave immediately.

Not wanting the rage directed at him, slowly, the cameraman backed out.

"Like I said, we have to be careful over the next few days. I don't see anything wrong with giving the Lou family soft condolences but other than that, stay out the way. We already got beef with Whoyawanmetabe. Let me handle the Lou's."

Bet looked over at Minnie and touched her hand. "How are you doing? With this Arlyndo situation?"

It was at that moment that all remembered that they were an item. In fact, the war itself began over their teenage love. Surely she should be broken up about his death.

Minnie looked down at her hand, which was clutched firmly in Shay's. Shrugging she said, "To be honest, I'm relieved."

That was cold.

There was a lower level in Banks' mansion and Whoyawanmetabe had discovered it.

As a result, Mason was tied to a chair, in the lock down room, a place Banks designed for specific purposes pertaining to the most private of matters.

Mason felt unsteady with the loss of his son and the mysterious man from Jamaica gave him little time to grieve. But it made sense. After all, he tried to take Whoyawanmetabe's life and in the end Mason lost his youngest son instead.

The mystery man was one step ahead.

Whoyawanmetabe learned earlier the day before that the sangria contained poison. The plan was given to him by one of his snoops who readily slept amongst the Wales, Nunez's and Lou families. Upon realizing that his life was in danger, he alone was responsible for switching the drinks causing Arlyndo to meet his early demise.

More would have died but most didn't want to take a chance on sipping the tainted concoction and for that they were alive.

Whoyawanmetabe, surrounded by his soldiers, walked up to Mason who was glaring his way. "Comfortable?"

"Ain't no cameras in here huh?" Mason said bearing teeth that seemed to grow in his mouth like fangs. "You got me in this bitch but don't want nobody seeing what's up in here."

"You try to kill me and I'm the bad guy?" Whoyawanmetabe said, crossing his arms over his chest. This was all amusement to him, better than sex if anybody bothered asking. "You should be kissing my feet that I'm not killing you and Rosa for the betrayal."

"My son dead. Do you understand? My son is dead and you don't give a fuck! You may have your reason for all of this but don't you got a soul? Huh? Are you really that fucking vicious?"

"Why should I care? It could've been me. It was supposed to be me. Let's face it, you played a game and you lost. One that you weren't equipped to weigh the risks. And it is for that reason alone that your youngest is dead." He chuckled once in the irony. "I mean come on...I tell you about my aunt's home made coconut sangria and you have your maid bitch make some up? Do you really think I'm that naive? Your plan was sloppy at best, don't you agree?"

Silence.

"So this is how it's going down." Whoyawanmetabe clasped his hands together. "You have three other sons." He lowered his brow and looked square down at Mason. "And you do love them right?"

Silence.

"Do you love them or not?" Whoyawanmetabe slammed a fist into a flat palm. It was obvious that his ego wouldn't allow any question dripping from his lips to go unanswered.

"Yeah." Mason said through clenched teeth. "I love all my children. Including the one you killed!"

What wasn't within view was as Whoyawanmetabe talked, Mason was quietly trying to get from up under the ropes that bound his hands behind the chair. What he wouldn't give to get at him. To lay hands on him and watch the breath be strangled from his lungs. Sure he would have to answer to his goons afterwards, who stayed with him at all times. But for sure it would be worth it.

"Then you will fall in line or I will see to it that your bloodline ends with you, on this island." Whoyawanmetabe walked toward the door.

"If you hate me so much, why save me in that prison? Why didn't you let the guards kill me?"

"It was all for this moment," he responded. Looking at his men he said, "He looks a little hot. Let him cool off one more night." He walked out humming an old Jamaican melody.

Howard, Derrick and Patterson were heated at the spilling of Lou blood on Wales Island as they paced their parent's bedroom. While Jersey on the other hand was so stiff as she sat sideways on the mattress, they wondered if she was having a nervous breakdown.

After all her son was just killed.

Where was her reaction?

Moments earlier they had returned from burying Arlyndo, on sacred ground, shown to them by Rosa Nunez and so they were still on edge. There was much to do before the sun rose.

First they washed the body, with the help of the Nunez family. The death ceremony was the only time Whoyawanmetabe granted them privacy, respecting culture as he did in his own country. He wouldn't dare mess with tradition and risk being haunted by ghosts all his Jamaican life. Next he allowed them to go with the Nunez family to the burial ground, but only with an escort.

Now back at the mansion, the Lou family was forced to deal with life without Arlyndo. "Sit down," Jersey told them, tiring of the agitated energy that surrounded her in the moment.

"Sit down?" Patterson said arms flaring at his sides. "Ma, you act like you don't even care!" His eyes were bloodshot red, as well as his brothers, due to non-stop crying.

"Yeah, ma, Arlyndo gone," Howard added as if all weren't already aware. "He gone! And you not saying nothing! Sitting over there like you dead too! I mean, what's wrong with you? Say something...anything!"

"Sit the fuck down!" She yelled louder, leaping up. "I will not be disrespected...not one more minute! Not by men I slid out my pussy!"

Hearing the rumble in her voice, a gift given from God to all black mothers, slowly they fumbled as they found available seats on the floor.

"I have sat by and watched as your father's antics caused two people to be killed in less than a week. One of them being my..." She broke down crying. "My baby boy."

Her sons got up to comfort her but she extended her hand and they returned to their positions on the floor. She didn't need their forced embraces.

"From here on out, I don't want anybody else in this family to make a move without me knowing. And I expect you all to listen, or else you will see another side of me. Don't believe me? Ask the two dead cops back in Maryland." She stormed out, reminding them about the recent bodies on her resume.

Whoyawanmetabe returned to the locked room in the morning only to see Mason staring directly at him. He hadn't been asleep since his son died and staying alone, locked down, drove him mad with screen shots in his mind of how Arlyndo desperately pulled for breath, only to learn that none was available.

To add to the misery, Whoyawanmetabe wouldn't allow any family members or friends to check on him while instead, assuring them, that he was okay in his personal care.

Sliding up to him in a flowing khaki colored linen short set, bare feet, his dreads were neatly tied back and it looked as if they were re-twisted although Mason couldn't imagine who would have taken on the chore. Of having him sit between their legs while they cared for his mane without killing him dead.

"You know, Banks doesn't respect you right?" Whoyawanmetabe said, rubbing his hands together like two logs trying to start a fire. "I'm probably telling you what you know already, but still."

Mason looked away, beyond irritated at this point. There was a spot on the wall that seemed to be separated from the wallpaper. It was a brown smudge that he focused on beyond all else. Besides, nothing he did seemed to make matters easier so he was trying to maintain control of his rage.

"Banks doesn't respect you because men like him," he paused and chuckled once. "...or women like him rather, think men like you and I are good for nothing more than muscle. Or goons. To protect them without realizing we want our due in life. We deserve it based on the protection we provide."

Mason faced him. "You killed my son. And all I wanna do is pay respects wherever he's buried. Can you let me do that? Please? I need to...I need to pray over his body."

"He can't be trusted, Mason," Whoyawanmetabe continued, ignoring his most basic desire. "Are you a glorified weapon? Or are you in fact dishonest and deserving of his disrespect?"

"Dishonest? Somebody could say the same thing about you."

"You see, it's expected for you not to trust me. I guess you can say that's why you attempted to take my life, even though all I wanted was to document your family. But for you not to be able to trust a friend that you've known all your life, well, that's different don't you think?"

"He's not my friend," Mason said through pinched lips.

Whoyawanmetabe smiled. "I guess you're smarter than I thought." He took a heavy breath that hung in his chest a few seconds longer. "I'll have one of my men release you in a few minutes. And out of respect for your son, no cameras for the next twenty-four hours. Consider this a gift from me to you."

A soft orange glow from the lamps caressed the space.

Mason sat on the couch in the cigar lounge drinking whiskey and smoking weed. He had spent the better part of the day at his son's grave followed by one of Whoyawanmetabe's goons, and his mind and heart were emotional wrecks. He hadn't even spoken to his family since the ordeal took place because the pain was too great. And since he was certain their agony was as grave as his own, he needed a break to be stronger for them.

And then there was the guilt of being the one to come up with such an atrocious plan that failed miserably.

At the end of the day Arlyndo's death was his fault.

Banks had warned him but he didn't respect his plea.

And now it was too late.

When Banks walked inside and saw Mason's face, Mason took a heavy breath. He had thought about him ever since realizing Whoyawanmetabe had taken him somewhat hostage below his house. His hair had grown a little longer than he liked and as a result, he pulled it up into a man's bun that gave whispers of the woman he used to be.

Pointing at the whiskey canteen Banks said, "You mind if I..."

Mason shrugged and sat back, glass in hand. "It's your shit."

Banks walked deeper inside and poured himself a drink. The brown liquor dripped into the glass like rich honey. "You remember when Arlyndo snuck them twins in the house that summer?" He took a sip and sat next to him. Mason had been tense for days and suddenly he relaxed in his presence. Just that quickly. Why did he have so much natural power over his heart? "I think he just broke his foot a few months before that. I'm not sure."

Mason chuckled once and shook his head. "Nah, it was the winter. Don't you remember? Because he was telling me which presents to take back because he already opened them all. Even the ones without his name on them."

"Fuck yeah!" Banks laughed heavier as the recollection hit his mind like a movie trailer. "He was carrying shit like a grown ass man. Like he wasn't eleven. Just destroying Christmas and shit!" Banks' laughter filled the room and caused Mason's heart to smile. "I mean he really thought he was gonna bone two girls right after he fucked up the holiday for everybody."

"He thought he was gonna hit them at the same time too," Mason said shaking his head. "Like where does he get this shit from?"

"Got mad at me too and everything when you dropped them off at home. I wasn't even there. Right before their parents called the cops at that!"

"Didn't speak to me for a week," Mason said still smiling.

"I was guilty by proxy." Banks added. They were clearly trying to make the moment last, knowing full well other matters would need to be discussed within the seconds to come. "I ain't gonna lie, to be young the boy had game."

They both laughed until it simmered like a teapot being taken off the stove. And for that moment Arlyndo wasn't dead, but a child somewhere in the world still living his life.

Silence became them a few minutes longer.

"I'm sorry, man," Banks said taking a deep breath followed by a huge sip.

His eyes rested on Mason who had to look away.

Because it was true.

Every rumor.

Everything Jersey said about his feelings for Banks was real.

At the end of the day he was still in love with the past after all this time. In fact he loved him more. And he hated Banks for not choosing to be what he was born to be, a woman, so that Banks could console him one more time.

"I can't get my mind around how it happened," Banks continued. "And I know you—"

"Like you give a fuck," Mason said from nowhere. Since Banks didn't choose to love him in the way he desired, he would rather anger sit between them heavily instead.

Banks frowned and sat his glass on the table. "Why, why you say that?"

"You never liked him." His nostrils flared. "I saw the look in your eyes when you saw him around Minnie. I felt the hate brewing just with the thought that the two of them could be a couple. He's gone now, Banks. No more need for the show."

"That's not—"

"Nigga, if you were gonna lie why the fuck even come in here? Ain't no need in being fake now that my son's gone."

"I didn't want him with Minnie but I liked him, Mason. You gotta know that. I fucking loved him like he was my own blood." A soft hand found it's way to his own heart.

Mason shook his head softly. He knew Banks cared for him. He cared for all his sons, despite all they'd been through. But it was easier being angry than it was being honest.

"I, I don't understand how my son is not here no more." He looked over at him with glassy eyes. "I'm not understanding, how, how I won't be able to see him again. Help me through this shit, Banks. Please, man. Or I'm gonna die."

Banks looked down, as if searching the floor for the proper thing to say. He decided he needed him in a different way, so he pulled him in for a deep hug and Mason was relaxed again until Banks said, "I know how you feel."

"How the fuck you know how I feel?"

Banks glared.

And in that moment, Mason remembered that Harris was killed not so long ago. In his grief, once again, he thought he was the only one. He took a deep breath. "I'm sorry...I...I..."

"You don't have to be sorry. I get it. The shit hurts and it don't get no easier, Mason. I didn't even get a chance to deal with my grief because something else is happening. And then I'm wondering if the other shit I'm facing right now is a blessing because without it, I'm left with blaming myself for...for...Harris' death too." Banks sighed. "I wouldn't want that for nobody. Especially not you. And I gotta be—"

"Strong for your wife and kids," Mason said finishing his sentence. "Even if there ain't nothing left to give."

"If you supposed to be strong for me..." Jersey said entering the lounge. "Then why are you in here? Why didn't you come see me after being gone for two days? Why Mason?" She sniffled. "I don't get any of this shit right now and it hurts! I begged that nigga to see you and you come here first?"

Mason swallowed all of his whiskey and poured another. "Not now, Jersey. I'm telling you I'm not in the mood."

"If not now then when?" She asked throwing her hands up in the air. "Tell me that at least!"

"Maybe I should leave," Banks said, standing up.

"No!" She yelled stopping his motions. "What I have to say you both need to hear." She took a deep breath.

Banks sat down.

But, Mason knew his wife and figured whatever she had to say would be too heavy for the moment. Or it wouldn't matter. He felt it best for her to kick rocks allowing her concerns to be voiced another day. "Jersey, I'll talk to you when I've had some time to think. I'll—"

"No! I, I lost a child too, Mason. And yet here I am, putting my feelings to the side to try and get through to you." She pointed at the door. "Because I have three other sons left and I want them to remain safe. I *need* them to stay safe."

Banks looked at Mason and then Jersey. "Go ahead and tell me what you want me to know."

"I know why he's here."

Banks stood up. "You...you do?"

She walked deeper inside and met him halfway. They resembled two lovers with so much to say to each other and so little time. "Yes, he's a fan." She looked at her husband. "Of Mason's."

Mason rose slowly but remained where he was not believing his ears. "A fan?"

How could that be? The man appeared to hate him.

The confusion was as thick as fog.

"I couldn't remember where I saw him from at first and then I recalled seeing him at your art show. It was the same night of the shoot out at Banks' house. The one that started the war."

Mason and Banks nodded, neither requiring details. The tragic day sat between them always.

"You were supposed to show up to the gallery but you told us to meet you at Banks' house instead," she continued. "So I left. We all did."

Mason ran his hand down his face. "Why didn't you say something earlier?" He yelled, looking to blame her as usual. "We could've dealt with this shit before! Fuck is wrong with you?"

Her face transformed from sad wife to that of a gladiator, ready to strike him dead where he stood. "How many times have I attempted to talk to you? How many times have I begged to be heard?"

"What you talking about now? I—"

"How many times, Mason?" She yelled cutting him off. "Only for you to brush me away like you always do? Like I don't matter! So don't come at me about why didn't I tell you when you never listen! You not even listening now."

Mason's chin weighed heavy and his eyes rested on the floor. "But, but this is different."

"How? You ignore everything I say. And every time you think I'm gonna have one minute of a serious conversation you scatter away like a roach. Not man enough to deal with it I guess.

You were going to do it again, tonight, but Banks intervened this time."

"I can't believe this shit," Mason said flopping down. He was under too much stress to handle the moment. It was best to let his wife and the true love of his life work things out.

He went for the bottle instead.

Banks walked closer to Jersey and held the top of her shoulders. Staring down at her he said, "Jersey, are you sure?"

She looked over at Mason who was pouring his feelings into the glass.

"Jersey," Banks said more forcefully, demanding her eyes rest on him. "Are you positive you saw him at one of Mason's art showings? I need you to be certain. And it's okay if you aren't."

"I...I think so." She looked down and then at her husband. "I mean, I know Mason doesn't believe me but—"

He rattled her again with a soft shake, forcing her eyes on him once more. He wanted facts and all other drama could rest. "I believe you. You hear me? I believe you. And all I want you to tell me right now is if you're sure or not."

She swallowed the lump in her throat as she thought about the night she saw him. It was one of Mason's biggest galleries as word had travelled through the underground that the man responsible for the controversial creations was selling new art. Made from the blood of his past victims.

All of the wicked in the land wanted a piece.

She was afraid to be right. Afraid to be responsible for whatever happened next. And yet there was a peace that came over her. Something told her that Banks would take the information and create the best plan to save her and her children. She was counting on it. She just hoped her husband would stay out of it and let the man work.

Looking into his eyes she said, "Banks, it was him. And I think he's been a fan for a long time but he looks different now. Maybe his dreads grew longer, I'm not sure. But I'm positive he was there the night of his last exhibition."

Banks hugged her tightly before quickly separating.

Mason, all the way drunk, on the other hand, wished it were he who Banks had embraced in his arms.

"Thank you, Jersey, that's all I needed to know." Banks ran out.

# CHAPTER FOURTEEN

Steam bubbled on the wooden panels in the sauna room as Joey and Cassandra sat inside. Joey wrapped in a towel around his waist and Cassandra's around her body. With everything going on in the mansion, they realized that the sauna was one of two places, the other being the Nunez's house, where cameras didn't roam.

If they did try to film there such high temperatures would destroy the devices.

Since hell broke loose in the house, Joey felt as if Cassandra was ignoring him. He wanted to not think of himself because he was feeling her, but it was hard because he wanted nothing other than to get closer. But where do you start when a person has lost so much?

"Cassandra, what's going on with you? I noticed lately you been trying to separate from me." He asked passionately. "Is it because of what happened to Arlyndo? Or that fight we had in your room? I didn't mean to hurt you again. I swear."

She sniffled and pat her nose with the balled up tissue in the palm of her hand that she always seemed to be carrying. It was so withered that little tissue balls rested wherever she traipsed.

"It's everything, Joey. Too much for me to talk about...maybe I...I don't know...maybe I just want to be left alone."

"So it's Arlyndo?" He pressed harder.

Having been born with a silver spoon, he was accustomed to asking questions and getting answers. Certainly he didn't want silence from a woman he was starting to adore, mainly because she didn't swoon like the women back home who learned he was rich.

"Yes. If that's what you want to hear."

Joey looked away and back into her face. "But you were like this before he died. All moody and stuff. I know we not together or whatever but, I'm here."

"I know but..."she cried harder. "But..."

"But what?" He asked as he touched her shoulder, causing her to jump. The apprehension she exhibited put him on edge. Something happened but what? "Talk to me. Did someone hurt you?"

She quickly rotated her head in his direction. "Just, just, leave me alone." She leapt up, grabbed her towel and rushed out crying.

"Fuck!" He said to himself, slamming back into the hot wall.

Taking a deep breath, and not feeling like staying, he walked out and right into Spacey bending the corner.

"You 'aight, man?" Spacey asked preparing to enter the sauna too. "I saw Cassandra take off a minute ago. Ya'll have a fight or something?"

"I'm fine," he sighed, wiping the sweat from his brow. "You know how these females be right?" He slapped his brother with the back of his hand trying to put on as if Cassandra was just another female when she was anything but in his book.

He was starting to *really* feel her.

"I know." Spacey sighed. "Arlyndo dying and this nigga in our house is enough to put everything off." He looked behind himself for a camera. Luckily there wasn't one in view. "But we gotta move through it you know? I mean, after Harris died anything else..." he took a deep breath and looked back again. "We can deal with anything."

"No cams today remember," Joey said wiping additional sweat off his face. "The Jamaican said it's to honor 'Lyndo." He frowned. "Like he knew the nigga."

"Or gave a fuck."

Silence spilled between the brothers and Joey was just about to walk off when Spacey said, "I think they raped...I mean, I think they raped Cassandra!" He blurted out.

Joey frowned, his head craning forward. "What you talking about?"

"I came past the bowling alley the other day. The nigga Howard was standing guard at the door and all of a sudden it flew open and Cassandra runs out. Clothes falling all off and shit."

Joey ran his hands down his face. "What the fuck is you talking about?"

"I just said it. Patterson was fixing his pants."

Joey's light skin reddened. "Why didn't you do something? What the fuck, man? You let these niggas rape a chick and all you do is stand by?"

Spacey's eyes widened. "What, me?"

"Yeah you, nigga! At the very least say something to me." He shook his head. "I could've did something and now look. Man, move out the way."

Spacey grabbed his arm and Joey snatched out of his grasp.

"Don't do nothing crazy," Spacey warned. "Now ain't the time to be starting no drama. You heard Pops. The cameras will be back and—"

"Don't tell me not to do shit." He pointed at him. "And I don't know why you scared of Howard after all these years either, but you better toughen the fuck up or else he gonna continue to run all over you, nigga." He stormed away.

She was lying across her bed when Joey stepped into her bedroom doorway. She had showered and was wearing a long white cotton nightgown. It was soft enough to showcase the outline of her body and he felt bad for wanting her sexually due to her grief.

But she was that sexy.

Her back was facing the door and he wasn't sure if she was awake.

Even though the cameramen rarely showed up in the Nunez's house, he looked behind him once before walking inside and closing the door behind himself.

She jumped when she heard him enter and sat on the edge of the bed. Clutching the drawstrings of her gown she sighed in relief.

It was just him.

"Joey, what are you...why are you here?"

"Did Patterson or Howard hurt you?"

Her eyes widened before she heaved heavily, falling onto the bed. "Please...just...just go away."

He sat on the edge of the mattress, so close that the tip of her toes brushed against the side of his leg. "You don't have to go through this alone. You don't have to suffer. Just give the word and I—"

"What?" She yelled sitting up. "You'll fight him? Kill him? I'm tired of all of this shit, Joey. I don't want any more violence right now. *Con el tiempo serás un recuerdo.*"

The hairs on the back of Joey's neck rose. He knew the saying in Spanish meant '*in time you will be a memory*' because she told him awhile back. What he didn't understand was why she kept saying it to him.

"Why you keep hitting me with that phrase? You said it to me once before, and your mother said it to me a little while after, when my pops was away. Why?"

"Joey, I'm not as helpless as I look. Leave me alone. It's not a request. You'd be wise to listen."

There was a darkness in her energy that changed her from a victim to a predator. He was forced again with the realization that there was a lot about the Nunez family that he didn't understand.

And that he wanted to stay as far away from pretty Cassandra as possible.

Banks had just gotten into a heated fight with Bet and made a decision that he no longer wanted her in their room. She had been acting strangely and since his mind was on keeping everybody safe, he didn't have the time. Luckily for them both they still had a half of day left without the cameras following.

They were in the midst of the argument about why he wanted her out when Jersey came running into the bedroom to alert Banks to what Mason was doing in the sunroom. "I'm sorry but I really need to talk to Banks." Jersey said, hanging in the doorway.

"Now is not a good time," Bet said, throwing a palm up in her direction.

"Bet, but it's important. I wouldn't be here if it weren't."

Bet threw up her hands and ran out of the room. There was no use in trying, he would leave with her she was certain. "What's wrong, Jersey?"

"Its Mason," she looked down. "I think he's about to do something crazy. Again. I'm so scared."

Banks hugged her. "Don't be. I have it."

When he walked into the den, Mason was painting a portrait of himself using his own blood and mud, a concoction he mastered and created long ago. Tiny cuts covered most of his skin because he hadn't punctured a vein, for fear too much blood would pour. He had to get creative. To place the painting, he had created a canvas made of wood and tightened bed sheets. Something he often did back at home.

By T. STYLES

"What are you...you doing, man?" Banks walked behind him as he watched him handle his paintbrushes effortlessly. He knew where this was going and he was so tired of asking him to fall the fuck back.

He was worse than five two year olds in church.

Mason looked back at him and continued to build. He was wearing a white t-shirt that was spackled with blood drops and dirt. The collar was sweaty, like he'd been running. "What it look like?"

Banks took a deep breath. "Mason, I know you think this the move but it's not." He inched closer. "And I'm begging you to let me handle this. After everything, you still can't trust me?"

Mason chuckled once. Thoughts of what Whoyawanmetabe said about Banks using him played in his mind. "You can't stand it can you?"

Banks frowned. "What you talking about?"

Mason's body grew rigid. "It bugs you that for once somebody wants something from me instead of you." He stroked wrinkles in the forehead on the canvas. "It burns you up that this man is a fan and that it's the only reason he's here. Not everything is about the great Banks Wales you know."

Banks looked at the painting and sighed. "Man, if I thought this would work, I would be here giving you my own blood. But it's not as simple as it may sound. I mean think about it. If he wanted a painting why not just ask? Why go through all of this?"

"Who knows why a nigga does anything." He shrugged and wiped his forehead with the back of his hand, leaving a blood smear. "Maybe he wanted to take a vacation too. I mean, you wouldn't know it with everything going on but we are in paradise remember?"

"Mason, so far every time I've warned you not to make a move, and you didn't heed my warning, shit didn't go as planned. Don't let your ego get in the way of facts again."

"So you blaming me for my son dying?" Mason asked, turning around. He was begging for a fight. "Is that what you saying?" His shoulders squared off and he was ready for battle.

"How come everything gotta be a war with you?"

"You the one coming in here all wrong. You not offering any useful scenario. Just telling me what I shouldn't do, even after my wife told you he was my fan. Not yours."

*Fuck is wrong with this guy?* Banks thought.

"Mason, listen, the cameras will be back later today. Let's use this time to make smart decisions together. Please."

Mason looked at him with hate, remembering all the times Banks broke him down emotionally, simply because he was weak for him. Simply because hew was more in love with him than ever. And in that moment he was starting to resent him in ways he didn't think were possible.

Picking up his brush he said, "This your house so I'ma say it like this, if you want shit to remain on a calm level between us, maybe you should step the fuck out my face."

"Mason—"

"Now!"

Banks shook his head slowly and walked out the door.

The cameras had returned.

And the Wales', Lou's and the Nunez's were seated around the table for dinner. It had been known as dinner theater because something was always happening. At the ends were Whoyawanmetabe and Banks as usual. Behind Mason was a large canvas covered with a sheet.

Everyone was afraid. Two people had died around dinnertime so not many were willing to speak or make a move.

Not only that, but the meal had been served and most did not eat, with the exception of Whoyawanmetabe and his men who always seemed to be hungry. After Arlyndo died due to poisoning, not many were willing to take another chance choosing instead to make their own prepared meals.

Since everyone was mostly silent, Whoyawanmetabe decided to be the first to speak. "So are you going to tell me what's under the sheet?" He asked Mason, wiping the corners of his mouth with a napkin.

Mason looked at Banks who looked away, and back at Whoyawanmetabe. Taking a deep breath, he stood up. The chair scraped against the marble floor. "I know why you're here, man. Stop playing games and keep it one hundred."

"What does that mean?"

"You know what it means." Mason shrugged, before dropping his shoulders abruptly. "Had I known before who you were I could've ended all of this earlier."

"I still don't follow."

"Come on, man," Mason said arrogantly. "My son died because of you. Spare me the fake shit. Once. Please!" He slapped his hands together and the sound popped loudly.

Whoyawanmetabe repositioned himself on the other side of the chair, his elbow sitting on the armrest. If nothing else Mason was entertaining. "Your son died because I was made aware of a plan to kill me. And in turn I counterattacked and he was murdered. In war, there are many casualties. Your son was one."

Mason's jaw twitched.

"What Mason is trying to say is—"

"Why do you do that?" Whoyawanmetabe snapped at Banks. "Why do you treat him as a child? In front of his family?"

"Treat him as a child?" Banks smirked. "I'm trying to tell you what he's saying."

"Why? He's cocky enough to say exactly what he feels." Whoyawanmetabe continued. "Besides, I sent two requests for you to talk to me privately and you've found a reason to deny me each time."

"I've been sick after the boy died." Banks said. "Not much in the mood."

"We will have a proper conversation soon, or things will get worse, *Mr.* Wales. I mean, you call yourself a man right? So what's the problem?"

Banks and everyone present caught the reference. In one sentence, he put on display Banks' primary insecurity. That people would look at him as anything other than the man he worked hard to become.

"I can speak for myself," Mason said to Banks. Taking a deep breath he focused back on Whoyawanmetabe. "I made something for you, something I'm sure you'll love. I remember where I saw you now. I know you're a fan so there's no need to lie. Consider it a gift."

When Mason whipped the sheet off, it exposed a painting of a portrait of his own face. He was in anguish and he'd even made tears coming down his cheek. Had it not been for the inspiration

184     

which everyone was certain was Arlyndo's death it would be a masterpiece.

"So, what do you think?" Mason asked Whoyawanmetabe, tucking his hands into his front pockets. "You like it or what?" He shrugged. "Are you gonna leave now?"

Whoyawanmetabe laughed. "What is it with you?"

Mason folded his arms across his chest, and then dropped them at his sides. "What you...what you talking about?"

"You thought this would do what for me?" Whoyawanmetabe got up and walked toward the other side of the table, closest to Mason. He ran his fingers over the painting, as if trying to determine if it were real. "You thought this would be strong enough to get me to go away?"

"I thought it would...I mean...give you..." Mason's words were lost in his throat where they should've stayed the entire time.

The man was so close to him that it was hard to maintain his emotions. He wanted to lay hands on him and was certain he could kill him with ease. But he heard Banks' voice playing on repeat in his mind. *Don't make any brash moves.*

Besides, they were out gunned and if something kicked off, his family could grow even shorter in seconds.

"Maybe Banks was right," Whoyawanmetabe said looking back at Banks and then at Mason. "Maybe he is needed to help you get your processes together, seeing as how you are clearly off without him."

Embarrassed, Mason looked at his family who looked away, unable to hold his gaze. "Listen, you want the painting or not?"

"No, a better question is this," Whoyawanmetabe said loudly looking at everyone. "Do you want to survive by participating in this film, or do you want to die right here and now?" His goons sat their cameras on the floor and closed in on the table. Removing weapons, guns were now drawn. "Because from here on out, if I get anything except for complete cooperation, there will be more casualties. I promise. Do I make myself clear?"

By T. STYLES

It was well after midnight in the dark kitchen. However a clear night and a bright moon provided just enough glow.

Banks was sitting on the kitchen table in the Nunez's servant quarters and within minutes, Jersey, Rosa and Tobias followed. The women looked afraid and confused on why the head of household chose to invite them without their spouses.

Tobias was suspicious too.

But since tensions had flared, they thought it best to trust him.

At least for now.

Besides, there was a common enemy.

"Banks, what is it?" Jersey whispered, looking behind him at the door for fear the cameramen were near.

"Yeah, this feels off," Tobias said.

"Don't worry. They never come in here plus it's after midnight." He sighed and ran a hand down his stressed face. "So I figure we have some time to talk before others get up in the middle of the night."

"So what is this about?" Rosa asked, moving closer. In the short period since she returned, she aged greatly after losing two daughters. So meetings like this did nothing for her cortisol levels.

"I know what he really wants and I need your help."

The women unknowingly held on to one another, sensing the worst.

"I guess it's not the painting after all," Jersey said, feeling sad she'd given him short news. "So sorry, Banks."

"Don't blame yourself. And I'm glad you told me who he was, Jersey. It helped. But now it's time for the next move. And I don't want you to be afraid, but you have to understand this is our only chance. And you'll have to keep this plan between us."

Jersey looked at Rosa. "We listening."

"If it's gonna get rid of him, I'm with you," Tobias added.

He had a different reason for complying. He just learned from Cassandra the night before that she was the one who told Whoyawanmetabe about the sangria. Her plan was to kill everyone but for now she was happy that at least one Lou was gone. She overheard the plan from her mother. As a result, he agreed to help, not

By T. STYLES

because of Banks Wales, but for Emetine.

"Alright, here's what we're going to do," Banks started.

# CHAPTER FIFTEEN

*T*his was another unusually warm and strange January day.

Her mouth tasted like a steamed seafood basket when Blakeslee kissed her lips. And her body was built like a woman much older than her fourteen-year-old age. At the end of the day, Blakeslee was disgusted. Still, as she sat on the step in front of her apartment building with the girl sitting on her lap, Blakeslee also felt more like a boy than ever.

When the building's door opened, Mason came out with sodas, sandwiches and chips on a plate. Since she hadn't eaten in hours, Cora jumped off of her lap and snatched a sandwich from his grasp before he could put everything down.

"Dang! Fuck is wrong with you?"

"Sorry, Mason. I was hungry." She sat on the step and spread her legs a little too wide as she continued to tear into the meal. "This turkey sandmich is so good!"

"Sandmich?" Mason shook his head and tapped Blakeslee on the shoulder. "Walk with me right quick."

By T. STYLES

Blakeslee followed him to the far end of the fence.

"So how's it going?" Mason grinned, rubbing his hands together. "You like her?" He knew she wouldn't but still.

"I don't know, man," she looked back at Cora and then Mason. "You sure your plan will work this time?"

"My plans always work."

Blakeslee considered all the trouble he caused her over her young life and quietly disagreed. Including how he tried to suborn her to steal a car, by bribing her with pizza. "Not really," she said shaking her head. "Remember the plan you had with having Hector mess with that girl at your party and then—"

"I know that one didn't go right but at least Nikki know how he is now." He shrugged. "Even if they still together, my plan kind of worked."

"I don't know, man." She rubbed the loose curls unraveling from her braids out of her face. "What if, what if Nikki see me with her and think we together?" She looked back at Cora who was eating another sandwich. "What if, what if she wanna get back with me but change her mind when she see that shit? That might make stuff worse right?"

"You gotta trust me," he smiled. "Nikki not gonna like this shit. So she got to come back to you."

Suddenly, from a far, Nikki could be seen walking toward the building with her twelve-year-old cousin Elena. Although they were almost the same age, Nikki and her aunt took care of her since her other aunt was on drugs. Nikki coming to the building wasn't a big deal, since she lived there too, but that didn't stop Blakeslee's heart from pulsing every time she saw her walk up.

Mason grinned. "Go sit with Cora. Real close and shit."

"Why?"

"Just go!"

Blakeslee walked away with her head down and plopped on the cool stoop next to Cora just as Nikki approached the fence. When she saw Blakeslee with her arm around Cora's shoulder she paused. "Elena, go in the house."

"But I wanna stay out too."

"Elena, go! It's too cold out here. Don't want you getting sick."

By T. STYLES

Elena trudged up the steps and past Cora and Blakeslee as she entered the building.

Staring at Blakeslee and Cora who appeared to be heavy in conversation and ignoring her, Nikki moved closer to Mason. "Who, who is that girl?"

Mason shrugged. "A friend...why?"

"How come I never saw her before?" She squinted to see how pretty she was from the distance. She deemed she was alright.

"You don't know everybody we cool with, Nik."

Nikki rolled her eyes and walked up to the duo. She would find out herself what was going on. "Blake, can I talk to you for a second? In private?"

"Why you wanna talk to him for?" Cora interrupted, a mouth full of food. "He with me now."

"Him?" Nikki said to herself. Although Blakeslee was doing a better job moving like a boy, she was a long way from being masculine, especially since her hair was still long.

"Blakeslee, please. Can we talk?"

Blakeslee was no match for Nikki's begging and she knew it. As hard as she was going she was bound to relent. Sighing, she stood up and walked into the building, with Nikki on her heels. "What's up?" She shrugged. "I was busy."

The moment the door closed Nikki cried in her arms. It was cool outside so she immediately felt the rush of her warm body against her own. This was intense. Blakeslee's heart jumped as she pulled her closer. They hadn't been this tight in forever so she felt woozy. "What's...what's wrong, Nikki?"

Nikki separated from her and wiped her tears away. Her face was blushed red with stress. "I broke up with Hector."

Blakeslee's eyes widened. "W...what...why?"

"Because he was cheating on me again. This time with Amanda. One of my friends." She shook her head. "I feel so stupid, Blakeslee. I feel like I knew he wasn't no good but still I kept taking him back."

Blakeslee moved closer and inhaled the mint of her breath. "You not stupid. He's the dumb one for doing you that way." She grabbed her hand and led her to the bottom step inside the building where they sat down. "I'm sorry that he hurt you. Again. But you'll get back with—"

"I'm never getting back with him!" She yelled cutting her off. "Ever." She sniffled. "And I know

194

I've said that before but this time I'm serious. He doesn't care about me. He doesn't even like me. So why should I keep—"

The door open and Cora appeared, interrupting their chit-chat. She scratched her sweaty underarm under her coat and sniffed her fingers. "You coming back outside, Blakeslee?"

"Give me a second," Blakeslee responded.

"Why you friends with her when she treat you so bad? She's—"

"I'm talking right now, Cora!" Blakeslee yelled.

Defeated, Cora slowly shut the door, looking at them the entire time, until the shut frame blocked her view. "You, you like her?"

Blakeslee shuffled a little on the step. "She cool."

Nikki exhaled. Feelings demolished. "Can you hang out with me today? Maybe, maybe we can order some food. I got some money from Hector. Didn't spend it all. I can use it on you if you want." Her eyes begged for attention.

"Why though? I mean, you can be friends with anybody else. Why you wanna spend time with me?"

"Because I miss you."

*That was all Blakeslee needed to hear.*

*For the next month, the two never left each other's sides. And although their relationship remained platonic, the bond grew thicker with time. Nikki finally realized how much she needed her in her life, and Blakeslee was on cloud nine just being in her presence. They finished each other's sentences without trying. Told each other scary stories in the basement of their building and screamed in fear. Walked to and from school together and when Hector tried to talk to Nikki, it was Blakeslee who blocked his way with a firm hand to his chest.*

*At the end of the day they just worked.*

*But that didn't mean everyone was happy about the reunion.*

*Once again, Mason had been outcast and it hurt. In the past, it was the three of them but Blakeslee was careful with the time she shared with Nikki now, afraid that he would do or say the wrong thing, which would push her relationship with Nikki backwards when she was making strides forward.*

*Nah.*

*Plans of their trio were over to hear Blakeslee tell it.*

By T. STYLES

It was now all about Nikki.

One day in particular things came to a head when Mason walked into the carry out only to see the two sharing a steak and cheese without him. Since Blakeslee never had money, he knew Nikki had foot the bill, which Mason had always took pride in doing. If Mason couldn't use his money, who was he to Blakeslee?

More importantly, how could he control her?

Instead of confronting them, and saying how much he missed Blakeslee, he exited; never making it known he was there.

"How are you?" Blakeslee asked, speaking from her heart as they continued to eat. "You seem kinda quiet lately."

"You mean about Hector?" Nikki said.

She shrugged. "Yeah, kinda."

"I don't care no more." Her mouth said the perfect words but her body mechanics whispered 'lies'. "I mean, he always get upset whenever we come here but he shouldn't have been cheating. It ain't my fault he—"

"Always?" Blakeslee stopped chewing. A pile of sub lie dead on her tongue like a ball of concrete. "You, you still talk to him?"

"Why you say that?"

"I mean, we only started coming here after ya'll broke up. So how he know about what we do now?" She grabbed a napkin and spit the food inside, unable to take anything more on her new sour stomach.

"Blakeslee, you and me are just friends," she said softly. "So I don't wanna spend time talking about him. Okay?"

*Just friends. Just friends. Just friends.*

Blakeslee chanted the words repeatedly in her mind, trying to find the underlying meaning. If she took her sentence at face value, understanding her words would be simple.

Nikki wasn't interested in anything but friendship.

And that shit hurt.

The next day, after getting out of school for a half day, Blakeslee was eager to get back home. Besides, she had big plans with Nikki that they talked about all week. It would start with watching MTV videos in her apartment, and end with watching scary movies over pizza and coke. Blakeslee even stole a five-dollar bill from her father while he slept, not wanting Nikki to always pay for their play dates.

*But why did time move so slowly?*

*As she sat in class, she literally counted the minutes on the clock until she could see Nikki's face. And then it happened. When the bell rang she jumped from her desk, knocking her seat on the floor in the process. Totally ignoring her teacher's demands to pick it up, when she ran into Nikki in the hallway, the expression on her face gave her chills.*

*Something was off.*

*Walking up to her, Blakeslee shivered. "Nikki, what's, what's wrong?"*

*"I got back with Hector."*

*Blakeslee stumbled backwards. "But...but...he hurt you. He made you cry and you promised, promised to never get back with him. You told me that. Don't you remember? Don't you remember saying that to me?"*

*Nikki looked down and when her hunched over shoulders caused the jacket she was holding in her arms to hit the floor, Blakeslee saw that it was Hector's. That meant they were together-together. "I know. And I'm sorry." She picked up the jacket. "But I gotta live my own life."*

"You said he embarrassed you by sitting at lunch with the girl and—"

"I know but—"

"But what?!" Blakeslee yelled, her light skin reddening. All of a sudden the other kids who were so eager to leave the building, now crowded around to see what caused the fuss. "You cried for a whole week, Nikki. Don't let him trick you." She stepped closer. "Please."

"I'm sorry. I really am. But even if you and me were to be together, it would never last. You a girl. Just like me and that's gross." She kissed her on the cheek and walked away.

# CHAPTER SIXTEEN

Whoyawanmetabe took liberties to light the fireplace in Banks' lounge. Whether he did it to relax the man who he called a meeting with, or to irritate him, was of no consequence to Banks.

Mr. Wales hated his guts.

Whoyawanmetabe sat on the left end of the sofa, stirring his whiskey via soft ice rocks in the glass. There was one cameraman in the corner, but most were out and about with other family members.

Annoyed, Banks walked into the room and took his position opposite of him in a recliner.

"I'm happy you agreed to talk to me." Whoyawanmetabe tilted his glass to his lips, allowing the alcohol to coat his tongue. "I know tensions are high so this means a lot to my cause."

Banks poured himself a drink and took a deep breath. "You have us where you want." He took a sip and sat back, allowing the soft leather to take shape of his body. "I don't see it as having much of a choice. Still, until you get what you want its best to be cordial." He raised his glass once.

The truth was, Banks had been faking not being available because he was afraid to have conversations alone with him. He believed that he was dead set on twisting an already destroyed relationship with Mason, which would ultimately cause Mason to make rash moves again.

Resulting in another person getting hurt.

"You know, as much as I look at you and I have looked at you long and hard. Both in passing and on the footage, I—"

"So you do review the recordings."

"Sometimes." He shrugged. "But what I find interesting is that I don't see the femininity in anything you do."

Banks' jaw twitched but he realized what he was doing. Trying to bait him. "Why would you? I'm all man."

Whoyawanmetabe offered a half smile that only rose on the right side of his face. "Maybe. In your eyes." He took another sip. "Banks, as you know everything we do in life comes with a choice. You ignored my request to talk in the past and then well, you know the rest. The house came undone and bad decisions were made. People died. That makes part of this your fault."

Banks rested his ankle on his knee. "What will happen now?"

"Hurt people, hurt people."

Banks chuckled once. "I don't think Maya Angelou meant it like that."

"Impressed. You read."

Banks' jaw twitched again. He was definitely well read. So he was tiring of the witty banter. "I'm here now. So what do you want with me?"

"I want to know what's happening with you and Mason."

The cameraman moved closer and Banks readjusted. "What you wanna hear?"

"The truth."

Banks took a deep breath. "If I'm being honest—"

"Please."

"If I'm being honest," Banks started again, "I'd say he's responsible for single handedly ruining my life. Has been doing this since we were kids. Always out of control, always making brash moves."

Whoyawanmetabe smiled. "Continue...please."

"I always felt like, like, I was somehow trying to protect him from himself, even if he thought he was protecting me instead." He placed the glass down on the table and rose. "You don't know how it feels to care about somebody so much but at the same time don't want to be around them. That's Mason. My reasons for not wanting his company have nothing to do with our past but everything to do with his erratic behavior."

Whoyawanmetabe leaned forward. "I can imagine how you feel."

"Can you?" Banks responded staring down at him. "This, this thing that Mason and I have together, whatever it is, is a gift and a curse. On one hand, I know no matter what happens in the world, its him and me. And on the other hand I know that no matter what happens fucked up in the world, it's him and me. We mixed in no matter what and I'm fucking tired! I want to be free of him for good." He clenched his teeth. "I want it to end and I'm starting not to care how it happens as long as it does."

Whoyawanmetabe smiled, as if he was preparing to eat a big juicy steak. "Have you talked to him? About how you feel?"

"We been at each other for over a year now. So much has happened that it ain't a lot of time left for talking about a nigga's feelings. We may have done that once we got to the island but you were here."

He took another seat. "Do you love him?"

Banks glared. "You enjoy disrespecting me don't you?"

"Why do you find the truth disrespectful? Why do you hide what's inside, with what's outside? You definitely look like a man but in the end you'll learn that it never works. And as far as Mason goes, you two are in love."

"You think you're smarter than you are."

"I'm rather intelligent."

"Are you?" Banks asked with a smile. "Because things don't always go as planned. You could make a wrong move."

"You know where threatening me got Mason. Do you really want to go there now?"

The cameraman lowered his device and touched the gun hump on his hip.

Banks cut his eyes toward the goon then back to Whoyawanmetabe. "Look at where we are." He raised his arms and dropped them at his sides. "I bought this place to live out my dreams with my family. Had it all planned out. And in the end I fucked up. I didn't consider people using my island as a prison to hold my family and myself hostage. And now look? I'm begging you for an escape."

"What ya'll in here talking about?" Mason asked walking through the door.

Banks knew the only reason he was there was to get liquor, which lately had been his pastime.

Whoyawanmetabe smiled and rose from the sofa. "Nothing that will interest you. He's too busy hiding the truth as usual." Whoyawanmetabe nodded at them both and walked out.

The cameraman remained.

"So you're friends with him now?" Mason walked over to the bar.

"Friendship doesn't interest me anymore." Banks sat down.

Mason chuckled once and poured himself a mixture of white and brown. Liquid death. "You say that now but that ain't what it look like."

"What do you want?" Banks crossed his arms over his chest.

Mason flopped on the opposite end of the sofa from him. "I wanna know why you in here talking to this mothafucka after he had my son killed? I wanna know why he so busy trying to hold a conversation with you without me?"

"You gotta ask him."

"But I'm asking you instead."

Banks smiled and shook his head. Mason was like a kid who liked to argue but worse. "I ain't got time for this shit, punk." Banks rose and moved toward the door. "Go somewhere else with that shit."

But Mason was still in his feelings. Placing his drink on the table he rushed over to him, yanking him by the wrist. "I'm talking to you!"

Banks turned around and shoved him with full palms to the chest. "Get the fuck back."

And so, Mason saw black.

Grabbing Banks with both hands, he knocked him against the side of the door. When Banks was down, Mason hit him in the face with a hard right. Still enraged, he crawled on top of him and hit him repeatedly in the face, as if trying to destroy his good looks.

Having a few inches over Mason, Banks did his best to block his blows but Mason's rage was relentless. In all the time they'd known each other, Mason never once dreamed of beating his best friend.

And yet there he was, welling on Banks as if he was a stranger on the street. He hated him for the past. He hated him for the present. And he hated him for the future he was certain would no longer include him.

The blows grew so violent that the cameraman dropped his gadget and ran to get help. It took four able bodied men to pull him off of Banks, who at this point was passed out, on the floor, in his own blood.

By T. STYLES

# CHAPTER SEVENTEEN

Bet sat on the side of the bed, over Banks, dabbing his battered face with alcohol drenched cotton balls. Each time she tapped a bruise, a lightning rod of agony shot coursed through his skin. "Bet," he groaned. "Be easy."

"I'm sorry," she tried to be a bit more careful as she tapped the next swollen nodule. "I know it hurts."

He sighed. "I'll be 'aight."

She shook her head and tossed a bloody cotton ball on the bed. "You always keep it together. How do you, how do you do that? I mean look at you. You're too red to be getting beat down like this. He could've killed you."

Banks touched one of the biggest knots on his forehead and moaned. "Falling apart never helped anything so why should I start now? Besides, the damage is done and now I have to deal with it."

"You know Mason well. What did you say to cause this much rage?"

"It's fine."

"I get that, it's just that, I mean, so much has happened and you seem like it never phases you."

He looked up at her. "Do you wanna phase me?"

"You know what I mean."

"Listen, Mason and I have fought before." He positioned his body so that his back was against the headboard.

"I get it but—"

"Why do you do that?" He asked harsher.

"Do what?"

"Make every moment into an interview? It's never enough to just sit in silence. You have to pry, push and poke a nigga until he snaps."

She dropped another bloodied cotton ball on the floor. "Maybe the real question is why do you pretend that nothing bothers you? Once, just once, I would love for you to feel something. Anything, Banks. So that I know you're real."

"There you go with this shit again." He shook his head. "Bet, I have one goal in mind. That's it, and I'm going to see to it that my plan is carried out."

"Well can you at least share your plan with me? Instead of acting like I'm too fragile to help? I am your wife."

By T. STYLES

Silence.

She lowered her gaze. "Banks...I am *still* your wife right?"

"Why you asking questions you know the answer to? Of course you my wife, Bet." He touched another bruise on his face. "Right now I just want a little peace." His hand dropped in his lap. "A little quiet so I can get through the next few days."

She rolled her eyes. "I know you not gonna tell me but what happens in the next few days?"

"Bet!"

"If you're worried about Whoyawanmetabe don't be. He always starts shit when he doesn't get what he wants."

Banks shook his head. She was annoying at best. "Have you spent time with the kids?" He asked. "I see you like a lot of alone time but they need you too."

Her eyes narrowed. "How you sound? Of course I spent time with the kids."

"When?" He ran his tongue inside the wall of his mouth, causing his cheek to bubble. He tasted more of his blood.

"The other day we were on the beach."

"I can't be responsible for them right now, Bet. I need you to step up until I get things together. Please."

She shook her head. "One of these days you'll stop hating me."

He frowned. Nothing about what he said indicated that he despised her and he saw it as just another way for her to fight him. She wanted something from Banks he was certain, but she wasn't built good enough to say what.

"I'm not doing this with you right now." He eased off the bed, face aching profusely. "But do what I asked."

"Or what, Banks Wales?" She tossed her arms up and they slammed into her thighs when she lowered them. "What you gonna do? Divorce me and then make me expose your secrets?"

He frowned and walked over to her. "Is that a threat?"

"I don't know, how 'bout you tell me?" She shrugged. "I will say this, getting rid of me won't be a good thing for you and your lifestyles. That's all I'm saying." She rose. "I'm not afraid of you anymore." She looked at his battered face. "Especially now."

He walked over to her and ran his knuckles down the side of her cheek, before squeezing her chin lightly. A slight grin on his face. "It would be a mistake to confuse this for anything other than what I choose it to be." He pointed at the bruises. "Tread lightly."

Half drunk after trying to destroy his long time friend, Mason was hungry. Wrecked with guilt that he came undone and further destroyed his life, he wasn't willing to admit to himself, his kids or his wife. After all, conceding that he was too brutal with Banks would prove the point that soaked the air in the mansion. And it was that Mason Louisville was unable to control himself.

His shame was so heavy; he took to sleeping in one of the guest rooms to avoid everyone, even his wife.

And now with the cameras away due to the late hour, he decided it was time to get something to eat. But when he bent the corner he was surprised to see Rosa, Tobias and Jersey sitting at the table, whispering. They all looked weak, with hunched over shoulders and were eating fresh fruit. Pitchers of fresh water on the table.

Were they coming down with something?

"The cameramen ate all the leftovers again," Rosa said to Mason, as if to pretend nothing was happening.

"What's going on in here?" Mason asked. He was suspicious immediately. They knew something and he wanted in.

Rosa tapped Tobias on the shoulder and they both walked slowly out.

"What are you doing in here?" Jersey asked with an attitude. "I haven't seen you since yesterday."

"I asked what was going on?" He looked back at the doorway and then his wife. "This feels off."

"Nothing is going on." She stood up and almost tumbled as she tried to get her footing together. Mason knew his wife well enough to realize she was hiding something. "I was just...just eating that's all."

"So you gonna lie to me?" He stepped closer. "All of a sudden you best friends with Rosa Nunez?"

"If I am lying, are you gonna beat me like you did Banks?" Her chin rose as if defying him, despite knowing that he was more than capable. After all, he took her down before in the same vicious way.

Mason's nostrils flared. He was already in his feelings about what happened with Banks so the last thing he needed was his wife making things worse by throwing his crimes in his face. "He had it coming. I should've done that shit a long time ago."

"You were wrong."

"You don't know the full story."

"What's there to know? I saw his fucking face, Mason! It was like, like you were trying to kill him or something." She moved closer, no more space between them. "Were you?"

"If I wanted him gone he'd be dead." He pulled out a chair and it scraped across the floor. He flopped down.

Jersey sat across from him. "It's not his fault you know."

"What you talking about now?" He grabbed a half peeled orange and pulled off a slice, stuffing it into his mouth roughly.

"My son is gone and the only person I can blame is sitting right in front of me. Banks had nothing to do with any of that part."

Mason stopped chewing and placed the rest of the orange down, wiping his mouth with the back of his hand. "You really wanna do this?"

"I'm just saying."

The air smelled of citrus fruit. "What's your thing with this nigga all of a sudden? Huh? "

"You drunk."

Glaring, he stood up and walked on the other side of the table, staring down at her. "You want me to ask again?" He cracked his knuckles. "What is your thing with Banks?"

She stood up and looked him over with the little confidence she could muster. "Look at you now." She shook her head. "It's easy to stay a monster when everyone has seen you after dark isn't it?"

"Jersey." His nostrils flared.

"Nothing's going on with me and Banks."

"You sure about that? Because I saw how you looked at him when he hugged you. The day you told him about Whoyawanmetabe."

"Banks listens."

He chuckled. "And I don't?"

By T. STYLES

"Nah. But I will say this, I still have a lot on my mind and fortunately for you, arguing ain't a priority in my life anymore."

"Fuck does that mean?"

"Mason, my Arlyndo is dead. Can't nothing touch me now. Not even you anymore." She smiled and walked away.

# CHAPTER EIGHTEEN

Spacey was bowling, something he thoroughly enjoyed because it helped him relax. In fact, Banks had created the room because he knew his son loved the sport so much. There was a method to Spacey's isolation. He noticed if he did his best to avoid human contact, the cameramen would get bored and go elsewhere.

And that's what he did.

Still, loneliness began to trap him, forcing him to think about the things he chose to forget. Like how Howard made him give him oral sex when he was twelve years old. Secondly every weekend they were at the house alone. No matter how often he begged Howard to leave him be, when the mood hit Howard, he always looked to Spacey to relieve the stress.

He had just rolled his fifteenth strike and was preparing to leave when Howard and Patterson entered with nothing but corruption in their eyes.

"You ain't going yet are you?" Patterson asked, slapping the bowling ball out of his hand, which slammed to the floor, missing Spacey's foot by inches.

Spacey went to catch the rolling ball before placing it back on the return unit. "Man, I ain't got time for this. I'm leaving before—"

"Play another game," Howard demanded, slamming his hand down on his shoulder. "Unless, you trying to be rude which you know I got a problem with." He gripped his dick.

When Spacey tried to cut left Patterson moved closer blocking all motions. "Wait, *are* you trying to be rude?" Patterson asked. "Like my brother said."

Spacey looked at them both and opened and closed his mouth. His voice was low and crackled. They were definitely on some bully shit. "Nah, I'm not..."

"What nigga?" Patterson said louder.

Spacey jumped while hating himself for being so vulnerable. So weak. "I said, I'm not trying to be rude."

"Good," Howard smiled clapping his hands together. "That means you get to go first."

With lowered shoulders, Spacey grabbed the ball he had been playing with and rolled it down the aisle. Knowing how much of a sore loser

Howard could be, he purposely left four pins standing.

"Aw, this nigga wack!" Howard yelled covering his mouth with his fist. "I'm 'bout to beat that ass like he my son."

"Nah, he just letting you win," Patterson said, rolling a ball and hitting all but one. "Like he do all the time."

Howard glared and scratched his scalp. "That ain't true! Stop lying."

Patterson, always the instigator walked up to Spacey. "Tell him the truth, Wales. You be letting him win so he don't get in that ass don't you?"

Howard and Patterson had always been brash but since Arlyndo died they were pure evil, like Mason.

Patterson's question brought Spacey great discomfort for another reason too. Did he know he was raping him with the comment *get in that ass*?

"Nah, I just be—"

"Roll again," Howard yelled, slapping him in the back of the head. He wanted to shut his brother up once and for all. He would've allowed Spacey to throw him a win but not if his brother was going to call him out. "And you better roll a strike too."

Spacey was confused as he picked the ball up from the return unit. He hated himself for being afraid and he hated himself for not being man enough to step to Howard and put an end to his misery.

In the moment, he silently prayed for an intervention of some sort but would it come?

Slowly Spacey rolled the ball down the aisle. He was so good that with little effort, he rolled a strike. When the pins crashed to their death, he looked at Howard who was enraged.

"See!" Patterson yelled, pointing a stiff finger in Howard's face, turning his dark chocolate skin red due to blood rushing to the surface. "He was letting you win!"

Howard's jaw twitched as he approached Spacey. "Do it again, nigga! Before I drop you." He wanted to prove it was a fluke and so he demanded a re-roll of sorts.

Spacey shuffled a little as Patterson laughed heartily in the background. Slowly he retrieved his ball and with zero effort, rolled it down the aisle again knocking them all down. Howard tried to do the same, but each time he left no less than three pins.

But Spacey, roll after roll, made nothing but strikes. His balls just hit different.

Howard, embarrassed beyond repair, was just about to hit him when two cameramen, hearing the commotion, entered the alley.

Not wanting to be filmed, Patterson grabbed the top of his pants and said, "Whelp, that's my cue." He bopped out.

Howard on the other hand walked up to Spacey. Placing his lips against his ear he said, "I'll see you tonight. Have that mouth ready."

# CHAPTER NINETEEN

Tobias rolled over in bed, only to see Minnie standing in the doorway. Confused, he popped up, but immediately felt dizzy when he did. The Wales loved using their right to go into any room they pleased because they owned the place.

So Tobias was a bit put off.

By this time, the bruises on his face had lightened although definitely still visible.

"Minnie, what are you, what are you doing in here?" He sat on the edge of the bed. "Something wrong?"

"I'm fine." She twiddled her fingertips. "Just haven't seen much of you that's all. Plus your mother, sister and father seem like you're sick all the time. Are you guys eating because—"

"We're coming down with something." He stood up and was a little off footing. The room felt as if it was spinning and he almost caught the floor. "But I'm about to take a shower. I'll..." He took another step and dropped like a lifeless bird.

Minnie rushed up to him and helped him back to the bed. "Tobias, you need to get help. I saw that clinical room in the back by the kitchen in this house. With all them supplies. You want me to get anything there?"

"I definitely can't leave." He said. "Ma goes to Emetine's grave and no less than one man is with her." His breath fell heavy. "This use to be such a beautiful place, well sort of."

She looked down, wondering what he meant. She looked over at him and placed a hand on his thigh. "You need relaxation. Let me help."

"What that mean?"

"Trust me." She smiled.

Minnie had run Tobias a bath and on her knees she was washing his back. Although the rag sat on his lap, hiding his dick, she had seen what he was packing a long time ago in the hot tub and thought it was the perfect addition to such a sexy body.

"...I wonder what we could have been, but in my heart, I always thought something would happen to him."

By T. STYLES

They had been talking about Arlyndo, something that always perplexed him. He saw her as such a calm person that he didn't understand how she could be with someone so off the hinges. He had no way of knowing that until she thought she would die in a ditch, that she was just as horrible.

If not worse.

He looked over at her and then back down to be sure he was still covered. "Why you say that?"

"Arlyndo always seemed like, like something was going to happen at any minute. It made me anxious and on edge. I could never be fully comfortable so sometimes I was just as bad as he was. It was easier I guess."

"Folie a deux." He said.

"A madness of two." She grinned.

He was impressed that she knew what the French statement meant.

"I've heard it said about us before and it was right. When we were together, we were not safe to be around. For anybody."

"Then why were you with him?"

"He was my first everything. I mean, he grew up rich too and he understood what it meant to be sheltered. We were always watched. Always protected and always bored. Except when we were with each other. Nobody knew we would get together. Thinking we were like brother and sister. But there was no one else; we had to fall in love. Had it not been for him I don't know if I would've survived."

He chuckled once. "Growing up rich don't sound like a problem to me. I grew up in the worst conditions."

"What you mean?"

"Everything we ate we grew. There was no such thing as extras because food had to be shared with everybody else on the land. Sometimes we helped the other neighbors but if things were scarce..." he took a deep breath. "Let's just say you'd be surprised what people do for survival."

She nodded her head in understanding. "I'm sorry. Here I am talking about how rich I am when—"

"Don't do that." He gave her his entire attention as he looked into her eyes. "Never apologize for being who you are. And if a man can't accept that, or feels inferior, he doesn't deserve you."

Between his accent and the way he spoke with his heart, she felt weak in his presence. She had to have him. Slowly she moved in to kiss him and at first he accepted before gently pushing her away.

"Don't be afraid." She smiled thinking it was that simple. "You don't have to worry. I want this too. I've been wanting this if I'm being honest." She tried to kiss him again but he pushed her back harder.

"No...I...I can't. I'm sorry. Not like this."

Her eyes widened as embarrassment hung over her shoulders like a cape. "Wow. I feel so...so stupid." She stood up.

"Minnie, it's not like—"

"I have to go." She dropped the other rag and it slapped against the floor as she ran out.

Spacey and Joey sat in the sauna, as sweat poured from every inch of their bodies. Both had towels wrapped around their waists as they leaned back into the wooden walls.

"...I don't know, man," Joey exhaled. "She still doesn't wanna talk to me. For the most part she stays at the Nunez's house. But I'm okay with that because I think something is up with her."

"What you mean?"

"I can't explain it but I got the feeling Cassandra is plotting revenge. On everybody."

"Well I don't blame her for staying alone," Spacey said. "The cameras don't like when you by yourself."

"How you feel about Pops having something planned?" He asked skipping the subject.

"I don't know, man," Spacey sighed. "I think this is one thing he won't be able to get from up under. With Whoyawanmetabe."

Joey frowned. "You act like you never met him before."

"I'm serious," Spacey sighed.

"Remember that time you were getting bullied at that school and—"

"I wasn't getting bullied," Spacey yelled, wiping sweat off his brow.

"I'm not trying to snap on you about getting punked. Just proving a point, relax." He shoved

228             By T. STYLES

him with his warm shoulder making Spacey sweatier. "Anyway, them brothers fucking terrorized you back then...and the fucked up shit it was a private school."

Spacey saw Howard's face in his mind. "Bullies be everywhere. Not just in school."

"Oh so now you admitting they were bullying you?"

"You gonna finish telling the story or not?" He frowned.

Joey laughed and used a hand towel to dabble the sweat off his brow again. "Like I was saying, they were fucking with you and after you told Pops, the next day they were changed. Went from trying to fight to—"

"Acting like my bodyguards," Spacey said finishing his sentence.

Joey laughed. "You can go to Pops about anything and he'll have an answer."

Spacey looked over at Joey, whose eyes were now closed as he took in the soothing sensation of the heat. "You really believe that?"

Joey opened his eyes. "What?"

"How you forget what we were talking about that quick?" He paused annoyed he had short-term memory. "Do you believe that if I tell dad anything, he'll have my back and not look down on me?"

"The man taught you how to fly a plane," Joey confirmed. "So I'ma have to say yes." He took a deep breath and tapped his shoulder with the back of his hand. "Well let me get out of here."

"What you think is up with Mason doing Pops like that?"

"They fight all the time." Joey shrugged.

"Not like this. His face is ruined."

"The better question is why the Nunez family been walking around like they coming down with something? Falling all over and shit." Joey continued. "I don't know if they faking sick for the cameras or if they scheming but they got me noid." He moved to walk out again.

"Stay a little longer."

"What's wrong with you?" Joey frowned. "You been trying to hang out with me all night."

"Ain't nothing up...I was..." Spacey looked down. It was useless. "Go 'head. Get out my face then."

"I'll catch you tomorrow. Maybe we can get into a fake fight for these cameras and shit since we been spending too much time alone."

Spacey nodded as Joey walked out the door.

Ten minutes later, he was going to leave too when suddenly the door opened and Howard walked in, a tight towel wrapped around his waist. Smiling, he flopped next to Spacey who moved over an inch.

Howard slid closer. Their skin connected.

Placing a heavy hand on Spacey's thigh he said, "Been a minute since you got me right? Don't you think it's time?"

Spacey swallowed the lump in his throat. For the moment he wondered why he allowed him to do things to him he couldn't tell a soul. Maybe he felt there was nothing he could do without making matters worse. Besides, Minnie and Arlyndo started a war.

What would Banks do if he learned a Lou was raping his son?

But something had to give. The evil in Howard seemed to be as easy as breathing. And Spacey always wondered what caused him to be that way.

"I'm about to go," Spacey said standing up.

"Sit down," Howard said through clenched teeth.

"But—"

"Now!"

Spacey took a seat and Howard rose. "You know what I want so stop wasting time before somebody come in here." He dropped the towel, exposing his already rock hard penis. "You want me to say it again?" He slammed his fist into his palm and his dick jerked.

Howard gave him a few seconds and then Spacey lie flat on his stomach, as Howard raised Spacey's towel and crawled on top of him from behind.

The moment he felt his heavy body on his, the weight appeared to squeeze tears from Spacey's eyes. Howard was brazen by his actions. Anyone could come in and yet he allowed extreme horniness and the hate he felt for being attracted to men, to make him so brazen.

Spacey would kill him if he could but he felt too embarrassed and too ashamed to react.

Turning his head to the other side, he tried to close his eyes as Howard tore into him. An animal, he grunted heavily while getting full pleasure all the while violating Spacey in the worst way. But something else happened in that moment.

232      By T. STYLES

Something that neither of them knew.

Mason had opened the door.

And seen it all.

*The high school's hallway was crowded as Mason walked up to Blakeslee's homeroom class. When the children had fanned out due to going to their scheduled classes, and he walked up to Mr. Merlyn's door, it had become obvious that she wasn't in school.*

*Wanting to talk to her because she had been avoiding him ever since Nikki got back with Hector, he decided to play hooky and go on a hunt. His mind journeyed to the many places she could be and then he remembered.*

*The last place he saw Nikki and her together.*

*Quickly he went to the carry out but to his surprise, Blakeslee wasn't there. He went to the park later but didn't find Blakeslee there either.*

*He decided to go to their building if nothing else worked because he figured if she was playing hooky, the last place she would be was home. When his search came up short, reluctantly he walked to their building but was halted when he saw his uncle sitting on the bottom step in the hallway drinking a can of beer.*

*It was cold outside but Mason was so frightened his forehead immediately glistened with sweat.*

*Larry smiled. "Wow, I didn't expect you home for another three hours." He looked at his watch before pouring all the beer down his throat. Thirst quenched, he crushed the can in his hand and sat it next to his foot.*

*Mason's heart beat different as he looked at the man who was supposed to be the fun part in his life. An uncle should've taught him things like how to talk to girls. And how to ride a bike and even fight for himself with the hands. He should've been keeping his most precious secrets. The ones his father would be too angry to listen to reason.*

*Yet they shared another truth unwanted by Mason.*

*Through him he learned how to have sex. And how to please a man. And so he hated him.*

*Mason turned around, his warm hand upon the cool building's door. He was preparing to go back*

234 By T. STYLES

to school when, "come here!" Larry said, rising to his feet. "Don't make me say it again."

Mason paused and turned around. "I gotta go to class."

"Nah. You already AWOL. Let's go upstairs," he said gripping himself long and hard. "I need a release." Instead of waiting, he turned around and trailed upwards.

It took a minute but Mason reluctantly followed. After being raped yet again by his uncle, Mason had to get away. He was sick of being used in such a horrible manner and the longer he got away with it, the more he felt like nobody cared.

If only he could tell somebody.

After walking with no direction in mind, he found himself at the bridge. The same one Blakeslee had jumped off that caused her back to be broken. After she was torn away from the love of her life.

To his surprise, she was there.

"What you, what you doing here?" Blakeslee asked.

Mason shrugged and approached her side, his warm hands on the cool gritty railing as he looked below. "I don't know."

She looked down too. "I come here some times."

He nodded. "Why?"

"Because I wonder what...I mean...if I died when I jumped what woulda happened to everybody else?"

"Shit would be fucked up."

She considered him closer. "Why you say that?"

"Because everybody need somebody to kick it with, Blakeslee." He shrugged. "Somebody you can talk to about stuff. You all I got or whatever. You may have been dead but I would've been fucked up out here without you. You can never do that again."

She nodded and squinted. Something was off with him and she quickly allowed Nikki's neglect to take a back seat in her mind. What was up with her friend? "Mason, are you, are you okay?"

Silence.

"Mason, you good?"

"I gotta...I got a situation that...I mean...something's happening and..." Mason felt himself on the verge of crying, which in his mind would've ruin his chances of ever being with her seriously. "...Do you think pain ever goes away? Like the worst shit that ever could happen...do you think it gets better, like, with time?"

By T. STYLES

Blakeslee looked over the bridge again. "I was sad all day. Like, mad about Nikki and..." She took a deep breath. Already growing tired of talking about her, of wanting her and not having the feelings returned. "...And then you came. And I'm cool now. Maybe that's all that matters. Maybe things get better when you got a good friend to talk to." She shrugged. "I don't know."

Mason considered what was happening in his life and how although he was experiencing the worst abuse imaginable maybe she was right.

Maybe that's all they needed was each other.

So he stood next to her until the sun went down, neither saying a word.

# CHAPTER TWENTY

Spacey had been isolated in his room ever since Howard sexually assaulted him. When he did leave his safe space, whenever Joey or Minnie tried to talk to him, he would quickly walk away, knowing that the cameras bothered single people rarely.

The mission was to be alone.

He also learned that Whoyawanmetabe had noticed this trend and had plans to force people together if the antics continued. Everyone was afraid of his threat, knowing he meant it. Still, for now, staying alone gave him peace.

So he was definitely shocked when he walked into the room only to see Mason sitting on the side of his bed. He could tell the moment he saw him that he'd been drinking. The scent of liquor wafted in the air like cheap cologne.

"What you...what you doing in my room, Uncle Mason?" He shuffled a bit. Even if Howard had not assaulted him, Spacey was scared to be around him, especially after what he'd done to his father.

"Sit down," Mason said, drinking whiskey straight from the bottle that sat between his legs.

Spacey pointed at the door with his thumb. "But I was going to the—"

"Sit down, nephew," Mason said harder. Although seriousness was in his voice, Spacey also detected compassion despite not knowing why. "Please."

"Okay, but we better hurry up," Spacey said complying. "I saw the cameramen in the hall looking for something to film. If it's all the same to you I don't want it to be us."

Mason positioned his body slightly to look at Spacey who sat on the mattress next to him. "What I'm about to tell you, I never told anybody. I mean, people may know of the situation, like my brother and Banks but I never gave details about how it made me feel. Until now. Until with you."

Spacey moved a little. "Okay."

"For most of my life, I was, was raped by my uncle."

Spacey's face flushed red and his chest hitched. Wanting to escape he jumped up and moved toward the door. There was no way he would let Mason rev up what he was trying his best to ignore.

"Spacey!" Mason yelled rising up. "Please stay. We have a lot to discuss before the cameras come. Because with or without them, I gotta say what's on my mind."

Spacey looked at Mason.

"Please, man." He continued.

His body felt weighted as he walked across from Mason, leaned against the wall and slid down.

Mason walked over and sat next to him.

"When I was younger, my uncle used to rape me. Two, three times a week." His head lowered as he looked down at the floor. "Even saying the words right now...even...even letting them leave my lips makes me dizzy with rage."

Spacey exhaled.

It was the first time he heard that someone else was experiencing what he had most of his life. Sure he knew others might have gone through sexual abuse, but never somebody this close. Mason was one of the most dangerous men alive and if he was raped maybe he, himself, wasn't weak after all.

So Spacey looked over at him. Was it possible that he was aware of what Howard had been doing to him all along?

"So..." his voice went too high and he cleared his throat to find his usual bass tone. "What did you do, Uncle Mason?"

"I made a decision that made shit final." He exhaled. "I killed him. And that's why, that's why talking to you about this puts me in a fucked up predicament. Because I know what it implies. But I don't want the rest of your life ruined like mine because somebody taking advantage of you. I don't want this thing...that's happened to you...by my...by my own flesh and blood." He gripped the neck of the whiskey bottle so hard Spacey was certain it would shatter. "I don't want the rest of your life destroyed by him. Something must be done."

*So he does know.* "What can I do?"

"Come with me." Mason sat the bottle on an end table and extended his hand.

Spacey looked at his fingertips and shook his head no softly. "I don't want my father finding out."

"It wasn't a request, nephew. Come with me. Now."

A few minutes later, they were standing in the bowling alley. A cameraman was following them after seeing them bounce down the hall with purpose. It didn't matter that he wasn't sure what sparked the vigor in their steps he just wanted the shot. And Mason was too focused to care if he trailed them or not.

When they walked into the alley, Howard was waiting.

"Why you had me stay in here, Pops? I was just about to leave." He smiled awkwardly, rolling eyes between his father and Spacey.

Ignoring his son, Mason looked at Spacey. "For you to heal, it starts right here."

Spacey's eyes widened. "What...what you talking about?"

"I can't make shit easier for you. Banks can't make shit easier for you. It has to be you...right here...right now. Finish it and move on with your life."

Spacey swallowed the lump in his throat and walked toward Howard. Nothing about his mannerisms said confidence.

"Fuck you want with me, nigga?" Howard barked confused on what was happening. "You running to my father and telling him I be whipping that ass?" He laughed again as he turned up the bravado for his Pops.

Doing his best to show off for him something Mason would have thought was cute in the past. Now he realized he had created a monster by making men who took instead of dealing with their issues. Just like him.

Mason looked at his own son as if he were a stranger.

If Spacey said anything to Mason Howard hoped it was about the fighting and not the raping.

Spacey looked back at Mason and then the cameraman who was waiting patiently for whatever was about to go down. Slowly his focus moved on Howard and something dark overcame him. He thought about the first time he made him do oral sex on him at a sleep over. Then again when he was using the bathroom only for Howard to enter and force him to his knees. He had a lot of pain and it needed an escape.

Why not take advantage of the moment with Mason at his side?

With everything built up, he hit Howard so hard his body spun around like a top before hitting the floor. Not expecting the blow to land with such precision, Howard quickly rose to his feet, lowered his body and charged; wrapping his arms around Spacey's lower legs, which brought him slamming down on his back.

The air was knocked out of Spacey's chest and halted his breath for a moment. But thinking quickly, Spacey used the opportunity to raise his upper body slightly, which allowed him to hammer on the side of Howard's face with closed fists repeatedly.

Howard, dazed and confused due to being struck in the temples, released him and crawled on top of Spacey instead. With this advantage, Howard pounded him repeatedly in the face until using all of his might; Spacey yelled out and jerked his body upwards, forcing Howard off of him like a bull bucks a rider.

And this is when things grew bloody.

Spacey thought about each rape and used the weight of the rage to seek his revenge.

Spacey landed blow after blow, which was so brutal, the cameraman looked to Mason, secretly wondering when he would bring an end to a massacre, which could kill another one of his sons.

But Mason remained planted. And feet rooted on the ground like a one hundred year old oak tree.

Because in the moment he was on Spacey's side as he watched him do what he wished he could have done to his uncle the first time he ever laid hands on him.

It took some time.

And the battle was not easy.

But in the end Spacey was victorious, standing over Howard's pummeled body as he rocked back and forth, begging for him to get up so he could drop him again. Clenched fists dangling like rocks. He could look down and tell he had weakened him not only physically but emotionally. He also knew that Howard would never come into his room again unwanted, or else he would be waiting to fight back.

"Never again." Spacey said mostly out of breath before spitting blood in Howard's face, which landed on his eyelids. "Never again."

Having proved his point, he and Mason walked away.

The next day Mason was sitting on the beach thinking about it all when Spacey walked up to him, taking a seat at his side.

"You good?" Mason asked, eyes still on the ocean.

Spacey nodded. "Don't tell my dad...about...what's been happening to me."

"Your father doesn't want—"

"Please, man. I...he got a lot going on and I don't want him to know about this. I'm begging you."

Mason took a deep breath. "Once you start holding secrets you can't stop. You know that right?"

"I'm not holding secrets. You know what happened. That's good enough for me."

Big facts.

They both took a deep breath, having finally worked through the worst experience in both of their lives, together. Mason had helped a young man who needed to face the darkest of demons, thereby helping to release his past demons too.

For the moment they both felt victorious.

And yet the horror was far from over.

# CHAPTER TWENTY-ONE

The fireplace crackled and the smell of burning wood sifted through the air in the lounge.

Mason was propped on the sofa when Howard walked inside, with a look of confusion to go along with the fresh bruises on his face. But more than it all, he wondered did his father know his vile secrets.

Secrets he wanted himself and Spacey to take to the grave.

"Pops, what you...what you doing?" His jaw clenched tightly, causing his teeth to grind with fear. *Does he know? Does he know about me?* With no answer, Howard walked further inside and poured himself a glass of liquor. "I overheard Banks telling ma we running low. On alcohol." He laughed. "I think they trying to say it's your fault. That nigga Banks owes us though right, Pops?"

Mason glared at him.

For the first time ever, Howard felt his father's hate steaming from his body. As a result, Howard felt queasy due to not eating, but drinking all day. It took everything in his power to build his self up to talk to him and now he was getting the reception he deserved.

He knows.

Howard took a deep breath with the glass clutched in his hand. "Can you believe Spacey trying to act like he hard? I could've killed that nigga if I wanted. He better be glad he's still—"

Mason got up, leaving his son alone.

Devastated, Howard flopped on the edge of the sofa realizing a man he adored knew his worst shame.

Walking down the hallway, Mason stopped where he saw Rosa, Tobias and Ives whispering. He always felt as if they were weird but so was everyone at that point. Not only that, his thoughts were so consumed with losing his son, that the last thing he was trying to do was figure out the Nunez's secrets when his world was falling apart.

He was about to walk to the beach when he saw Banks and Jersey whispering in a guest room. And when he saw the burgundy circles encompassing mounted bumps on Banks' face, caused by him, it shocked him still. He hadn't seen him since the fight and so was now faced with how badly he injured his old friend.

Still, what was he doing with his wife?

Banks' hands were on her shoulders and she was looking up at him in a way she never had with Mason. Her entire attention seemed to be zoomed in on every word as if she was his lover, waiting on him to lead the way.

Confused, Mason backed up and looked downward with thick long breaths. He was trying desperately to calm himself, to prevent making another brash move.

It didn't work.

Letting his feelings take the reigns, he stormed inside; fists clenched and ready to fight again. "What's, what's going on in here?"

They separated from each other quickly, a soft glow of guilt on their faces. "I'll talk to you later, Jersey." Banks said exiting the room without saying a word to Mason.

Jersey took a deep breath and walked up to her husband. Arms crossed over her small breasts. "Are you gonna tell me why Spacey and Howard were fighting now?"

Mason frowned. "Is that what's going on with you and Banks? Ya'll talking about the kids?"

"I don't know if he knows," she shrugged. "Spacey told Banks they got into it over bowling. But I know it's not the truth." She tucked a small piece of hair behind her ear.

"Then what's going on with you and Banks?" His nostrils flared. "Why ya'll in here alone?"

"What you mean?" Her feet shuffled under her body.

And suddenly it was as if someone had dimmed the lights and he was in space. He blinked and Mason took a deep breath, trying to stay in the present. Why was she ignoring him? "You know, I swore I'd never lay hands on you again. And I'm trying hard to keep my promise, but if you don't answer my question you gonna make me drop you." He stepped closer. "Please don't make me do it. I'm trying hard over here."

She stepped back from his rage. "We weren't talking about anything."

"So why the fuck is you looking up at him like, like you want something from him?"

"Banks is easy going, Mason. And I just lost Arlyndo. He lost Harris and we get each other. That's it." She flopped on the bed. "I don't understand why it's such a big deal anyway. You don't sleep in our room. You don't talk to me." She shrugged. "So what difference does it make if someone else consoles me a little around here?"

The cameraman entered the doorway.

Mason looked back at him and ran a hand down his sweaty face. Why were they every fucking where? Filming. Watching. Catching the shot. It was as if they were trying to drive him mad.

It wasn't until that moment that he realized he was perspiring. "Banks is fucking with my head right now."

She frowned. "How?"

"I don't know, but, but I don't trust him. At one point he was the only person I trusted in the world and now...now I don't want him nowhere near me. My wife. My kids."

The cameraman walked closer eager to catch each word.

Mason looked back at him and took a deep breath. "Until I figure shit out," he continued, "Stay away from him."

"Tell me something, who are you jealous of, me or him?" She walked out.

If he had gone to a doctor, Mason would be labeled legally insane.

Still, it was easy to see why.

Arlyndo, the son most like him was dead. He found his other son raping the son of his best friend. And then, his heart told him that Jersey and Banks were getting a little closer than necessary.

Could they be having an affair?

Sitting on the beach, he was on his final cup of liquor, the last cup in the house, when Bet walked outside. She was wearing a white see through sarong that showed the gold swimsuit - she was wearing underneath. Her disposition screamed desperation and she didn't care. She had hoped Tobias would be interested in a little pussy but his attention appeared to be with trying to get her daughter to talk to him, although she didn't know how they fell out.

"Mason, are you okay?" She asked, standing over top of him.

He looked up at her and felt his dick jump in his jeans. Whenever anger consumed him sex was near and now was no different. She was basically showing him her body.

He averted his attention on the ocean. "Just, just trying to..."

"Get away from the cameras?" She smiled, sitting down. She was so close had he moved a limb they would be connected by flesh.

He nodded. "So how are you and Banks?" His question was heavy with reasoning.

She shrugged. "Banks doesn't want me in his bedroom. He's been acting weird ever since he spoke with Whoyawanmetabe and I don't know why. So for now I'm just here."

He smiled. "You sound like me."

She took a deep breath and allowed the fresh air to traipse through her lungs. "Mason, are you still, are you still in love with Banks?"

He laughed.

By T. STYLES

She turned toward him. "I'd really like an answer."

He shook his head due to tiring of answering the question. Yes he loved him in a way he shouldn't but he was certain the people around him knew already.

"Banks was somebody I could always see, see myself in. I mean, even when shit kicked off, and the war started, I knew we would go through it together because, that's the way it had always been. We got history and I felt like, like I could always count on him to be who he was. To be my friend."

"You talk in past tense. Why?"

"Things changed." He sighed.

"Is that why you hit him the way that you did?"

"I lost it. I guess everyone was right after all." He shrugged. "My temper is off the hinges. And to be honest I don't give a fuck anymore. For real, I'm tired of talking about it."

"You can talk to me, Mason. And I know, I know Banks makes it out that I can't handle much but I can handle more than he gives me credit for. We haven't even slept in the room together since I cleaned his bruises. He won't even let me touch him. Says he needs his space. And I need somebody to talk to. Will you talk to me?" She begged with her eyes and he looked away.

"What about the kids?"

"Minnie's involved in this strange tug of war with Tobias. Spacey and Joey seem to spend a lot of time together and Shay and Derrick are close now although they try to hide it. So trust me when I say, I'm alone."

Mason looked behind him for the cameramen and buried his glass in the sand when he didn't see one near. "Let's go to the towel shack."

"For what?" She smiled.

*Let's not play games.* He thought. *You been throwing that pussy around for days.*

"In case a cameraman comes." His eyes said he wanted more and he felt she did too. "We going or not?"

Slowly they both rose, eyes planted on one another. Once on their feet they hurriedly moved toward the towel shack. Now inside, they walked to the far back, where Mason used to sleep when Banks didn't know he was on his island.

Passion and lust were in the air. As thick as a dense forest.

The moment they were alone, Bet rushed up to him and kissed him deeply, tongue slithering into his mouth. It was a clumsy action that caused the air to rush from his body the moment their frames connected. But she was just so horny.

If someone asked him before this moment, he would swear he had no clue she would react this way. But deep in his soul, he was quite aware that she longed for companionship. It was mixed in the natural scent permeating from her pussy and the coconut shampoo in her hair. It was mixed in the way her eyes always searched for attention whether it be from Banks, himself or even the cameramen.

And despite having a wife desperate for attention himself, Mason chose to humor his best friend's spouse by fucking her raw instead.

Ready to push inside of her, there was a towel rack near and he shoved the linen to the floor. He lifted her up and plopped her on the table so that her pussy covered his bulging dick and her legs dangled around his waist. Tearing at her clothes he shoved greedily into her warmth as her head fell back in awe.

Their mutual hate for Banks in the moment made this the most passionate sex either of them experienced in a long time. In and out of her body he went and before long their chemistry born a thin strand of oil that oozed out of her pussy and dampened the wood beneath her.

Placing his lips against the crease of her neck, he breathed in deeply as if she belonged to him. She smelled like lust. Like disrespect. Like hate and he needed her more than he realized because of these things.

"You feel so good," Bet said scratching at his back with nails that dug deeply into his skin, leaving with them their secrets.

"I'm fucking you better than Banks?" He asked through forced breath.

"Better...better!"

"You been wanting this dick, huh, you been needing this dick." He said, feeling himself growing hot at fucking a woman that belonged to Banks. It was as if by being with her, he was fucking him instead.

"I been needing this dick for a long time," she said before kissing him heavily. "You feel so—."

"Mason," Jersey said standing in the doorway. "What...what are you doing?"

Mason pulled out of Bet's wet pussy and turned around. When he realized he was still exposed, dripping with the juices of his best friend's wife, he tucked his dick away. "I...it's..."

There was no use in lying and he knew it, he was caught.

Jersey's eyes fell on him and then Bet. "Oh my, God! Oh my..." She covered her mouth and ran out, stumbling in the sand in the process.

"Jersey!" Mason gripped at the hem of his pants but fell over on his way to catch her. Instead he met the ground quickly.

When he first entered his best friend's wife it was due to the many emotions playing tricks on him. But now with Jersey holding a secret he knew would destroy him and Banks' relationship forever, suddenly he realized the hate he had for Banks didn't reach as deep as he thought. Now he understood that he secretly hoped their bond would return to normal. But if this got out it would be impossible.

He had to stop her.

By any means.

But there was one problem.

The alcohol he had been drinking earlier caused his equilibrium to be off. And so he crashed face first into the sand as he ran toward the mansion.

But Jersey was quick.

Jersey was angry and he was nowhere near the bearer of bad news.

Picking himself up again, he hobbled back to his feet as he gave a faster chase. "Jersey!" He yelled bare feet covered with sand running through the hallways. "J...Jersey, please don't tell him! It'll destroy us! Please, baby!" Normally they rinsed their feet at the footbath by the front entrance outside of the mansion to avoid trailing sand inside, but there was no time.

Mason was so loud as he tried to stop her, that all of the cameramen quickly rushed behind him eager to get the shot.

By T. STYLES

Minutes later, Banks ran up to Jersey who was just exiting her room. "What's wrong?" He held her by both forearms. "Are you hurt?"

"Move out my way, Banks!" She rushed past him and headed for his bedroom.

But he caught her and grabbed her again. "Please don't do anything crazy. Remember the plan."

"Fuck your plan!" She yelled louder. "I'M SICK OF EVERYTHING AND EVERYBODY IN THIS MANSION!"

Banks blinked several times.

When he glanced down, he could see she was concealing something in the front of her waist. He yanked her arm. "Jersey, fuck is happening? Talk to me! "

She wiggled out of his grasp as she stormed into his bedroom. Once there, she saw Bet standing in the middle of the room with a towel wrapped around her body. Her feet covered with sand. Guilt written all over her face.

The moment Bet saw Jersey, followed by Mason, Banks and three cameramen, she felt weak in the knees.

This would undoubtedly be a show.

Jersey stared at Bet trembling with rage. "How, how could you do something like that to another woman? What is wrong with you? What kind of person are you?"

Bet's two white palms faced her direction trying to hold her back. "Jersey, I'm so sorry," she said, trembling. "It all happened so quickly and...and I fucked up. I wish I could take it back but I fucked up."

"Wait...what's...what's going on again?" Banks asked his fists planted in the crease of his waist.

Jersey looked back at him, just as Rosa and Tobias Nunez walked inside. Both of them stood next to Banks.

"Is everything okay, Mr. Wales?" Rosa asked.

There were so many people inside the room it was tough to breathe. "Just go to your house, Rosa," he said. "Everything is—"

"Answer me!" Jersey yelled at Bet, reminding all why the crowd had assembled. At the end of the day she caught her husband with another woman and she wanted answers.

Bet opened and closed her mouth. "I...I'm sorry." She shrugged as weak tears trailed the length of her cheek, dangling on her chin like morning dew. "I really am."

Banks stepped closer to his wife. "Bet, what did you do?" He scratched his scalp.

"She fucked Mason," Jersey said crying. "I caught them in the towel shack."

Banks opened and closed his mouth. Slowly he looked over at Mason, heart tilted back upon hearing the news. "Is this...is this true?"

"I'm sorry, man, I...I been fucked up for awhile and...and...there's no excuse. I swear to God I wish I could take it all back but I can't. I can't, man and I'm sorry. Banks, please lets talk about this...alone."

Before Banks could respond Jersey whipped out a gun and aimed it at Bet. "Yeah...well...I'm sorry too."

Banks quickly pushed Bet to the side and everyone screamed as Jersey squeezed the trigger and Banks had received a bullet for his efforts.

In that moment, Mason's life flashed before his eyes as he leapt over the bed to help his friend.

The room was in complete pandemonium as two of the three cameramen tackled Jersey to remove the gun. They were in shock. After all, they thought they confiscated all weapons.

It was cool though.

Because one cameraman kept focus, and he got the, shot.

Mason sat in the kitchen staring out into space. His eyes were so blurry from tears; it was as if he had gone blind. His entire world was rocked yet again as another fear was realized.

*Banks Wales was gone.*

He was still replaying the bullet Banks took repeatedly in his mind, as Whoyawanmetabe strolled up to him, hands tucked in his pocket just as cool as chilled water.

Slowly Mason's head rotated in his direction. "Now is not the time," Mason warned with a deep throaty voice.

He shrugged. "I think it is though."

Mason looked down, rubbed his reddened eyes and breathed heavily. "My friend is dead and you coming in here to say what to me right now?" He asked through clenched teeth. "If I were you I'd

By T. STYLES

tread lightly because for real, I don't give a fuck anymore. And that includes about living."

"I will leave you your time in a minute. As I honored the no camera policy for your son, I will do the same for your friend, for two days."

Mason could care the fuck less. He was trying to survive the next minute, let alone the next day.

"I understand how it feels to lose somebody you love," Whoyawanmetabe continued. "My aunt, that I was telling you about, she was the closest person in my life until she died and I met a woman. Because of my lady it changed the course of everything I did. She left me too though. But when I lost her I made it my business to learn different languages and I travelled the world." His expression was far off.

"Again, what the fuck do you want from me?"

Whoyawanmetabe blinked several times and took a deep breath as he returned to the present. "You're in pain, Mason Louisville. Use it. That's all I'm saying." Whoyawanmetabe smiled as he walked out the door.

# CHAPTER TWENTY-TWO

The air had been sucked from the mansion.

All hope was officially lost.

Minnie, Joey and Spacey sat on the living room sofa as Bet stood before them, a complete wreck. Living without Banks was not something the Wales family was prepared to do and yet it looked as if they would have no choice. The man with the plan. The protector of the family.

Their rock.

*Dead.*

"So, this is, this is all your fault?" Minnie said in a quiet hate filled whisper. Her gaze on the floor. Eyes bloodshot red. It seemed like forever but eventually her focus rested on her mother. "That's what you're telling us?"

"I...I didn't..." Bet tried to formulate the words but nothing worthy of speaking exited her lips. She had been caught fucking his best friend and as a result Banks was shot. While trying to save her life at that. "I didn't know I...I didn't know this would happen."

"You took the one person, the one person who, whose only crime was...was...keeping us safe!"

Minnie yelled leaping up. "How could you? How could you do this to all of us? We can't even get off this island without him. He was our everything and...and...now..."

"I didn't know she would...she would try to kill me," Bet cried. "I...I was...out of my mind and..."

"Stop making fucking excuses!" Minnie tore into her like the end of a recently sharpened blade to soft flesh. "Nothing you say will matter ever again!"

Bet walked over to Minnie, in an attempt to soothe her with touch. For her efforts she was shoved roughly away. Bet grabbed her once more and now with her mother upon her, she used the moment to hit her blow after blow in the arms, chest and face. It took Spacey and Joey to hold her back.

But Minnie shook them off as she ran toward the door. Before leaving she stopped and slowly turned around. As if she realized something. Something of great importance. "I'm...I'm not running anymore," she said, wiping tears roughly from her eyes. "You leave." Her gaze was firmly on Bet as she crossed arms over her chest.

Bet was stunned, feet planted in the marble floor like nails to wood.

"Minnie, don't come down on ma like this," Spacey said. "It's not her—"

"GET OUT!" Minnie yelled at her mother. "I don't want to see your face! Ever!"

He was in his room...alone.

Mason used the moonlight from an open window to paint his newest creation. Dried tearstains rusted his cheeks as he dipped his brush into a bucket of Banks' blood.

Although Mason didn't know it, due to being engrossed in his work, Whoyawanmetabe stood in the doorway as he watched the painting take shape. This was the moment Whoyawanmetabe had been waiting on. A painting not only derived out of pain but from the blood of his most precious friend.

Banks Wales.

By T. STYLES

Which meant in the underground world its worth would be far more than the canvas it was painted on.

With finally getting what he desired, he walked quietly out the door, closing it behind himself.

When Whoyawanmetabe walked toward Banks' room, he opened the door slightly when he heard prayer in Latin. Rosa, Tobias and Roxana stood around Banks' grayed out body lying on the bed. There was so much blood it colored the cream sheets burgundy.

"How is everything?" Whoyawanmetabe whispered trying to get a good view.

Rosa glared. "We have given you everything you've asked. Please, leave us be while we prepare his body. Don't disrespect his spirit." She warned. "It wouldn't be good."

Whoyawanmetabe wasn't scared of a lot, but being hunted by the dead was one of them. And so he nodded and walked out.

# CHAPTER TWENTY-THREE

All the curtains were drawn but the light of the Himalayan orange salt lamps lit the space.

Whoyawanmetabe sat at a desk in his room his back faced the door. When Bet walked inside he smiled before even seeing her because he knew she was there. She had a standing invitation since he arrived to the island but she never saw fit to use it until now.

Curious, he turned around in the chair. "So now that he's gone you know who I am?" He rose to his feet. "All of a sudden you remember our past? All of a sudden you remember me?"

"The guards let me in." Her eyes were as red as merlot and she was wearing blue jeans and a white shirt that was ripped in many places.

He shrugged. "That's because I told them to always allow you entry."

"What have you done?" Her words slithered out in a heavy hush. "You...you caused him to be killed."

He frowned. "You come at me with this?" He pointed at himself. "After you left me for him?

After I put you through school to be a realtor? After you promised to marry me and destroyed my world in one breath? You didn't even say goodbye when you left our home. That we purchased...together."

"I didn't leave you I—"

"You knew I was a fan of Mason's work! And like you do everything else in life, you obsessed on him first."

"I didn't obsess." She crossed her arms.

"You fucking followed him, Bethany. You followed Mason and was going to make your move on him. But then you saw Banks when he was home one day from Texas, didn't you? And you set your sights on him instead. Even introduced yourself to his father so you'd be able to sell both of them their houses. I know your full story so stop the lies."

She looked down. "I never promised to marry you!" Was all she could utter upon hearing the truth be rattled like broken glass. "And now none of it matters because Banks is dead."

"You broke my heart to be with a woman." He shook his head. "What kind of abomination is that?" He walked closer. "And then what happens? The moment he abandons you on this fucking island and you thought he wasn't coming back to save you, who was the first person you called? Me!"

"What about you? What about making your violent services available to Linden just so you could get a connection with Banks and Mason? Just so you could get back at me."

"I did whatever I had to do and now I have that and so much more."

Her chin rose and her chest seemed to widen. "I'm not going to be with you, Delray. Even...even with Banks dead I'm not...not going to be with you."

He glared slowly. "I don't want you anymore." He chuckled. "You're tainted anyway. So it was never about that with me." He looked at her feet as if he was preparing to spit on them.

She readjusted her stance, crossing her arms at her chest. "Then what *do* you want?"

"That niggas blood," he shrugged. "On my painting. And I'll have that and so much more." A smile took up his entire face.

"So filming us was all a ruse?"

"What do you think?"

"I hate you so much." She whispered.

"And I loved you, until you broke a promise and used me to build a career. I mean, don't you understand what kind of man I am? Don't you realize how far I would go to ruin the life you built? Even if it took me twenty years. You did this, not me." He walked up to her and caressed the side of her face. His hand cool upon touch. "Think about that as your children hate you for the rest of your life. I know I will."

The table was set but not for dinner.

Not this time.

The dining room was dark when Whoyawanmetabe strutted inside, without his men. With the exception of a lit candelabra on the table next to where Mason sat, there was limited glow. But it was the object behind Mason that drew Whoyawanmetabe's attention and caused his mouth to water.

It was covered in a sheet.

As if waiting on him like the body of a beautiful naked woman.

Slowly Whoyawanmetabe moved toward it, as smooth as if he were gliding on rollerblades. He savored every moment, before even seeing the work of art.

Mason took a deep breath and looked down at his clutched hands. "Why the cameras?"

"Excuse me."

He focused on him. "This is what you always wanted, for me to kill my best friend and use his blood to paint so why...why the cameras?"

Whoyawanmetabe smiled. "You know, it's funny. When people know they are being filmed, at first, they are robotic, unnatural. But with some time, they come to look at the cameras as a priest of sorts. A source for them to display their darkest confessions. I knew what I wanted and I knew what things to put in place to get me there. I needed extreme chaos. I needed you and Banks to despise each other. In one location. So the cameras were a diversion."

"But why film everybody? Why not just me and Banks?"

"Because Banks was smart. He would've caught on."

274  By T. STYLES

Mason looked down and shook his head slowly. "You know, when I first found out you had a connection with me in some way, I was cocky. True. Figuring...figuring I could...could give you what I thought you wanted and...and you would leave." His rage was quiet and contained, unlike the recent past. "If only I could see what you wanted all along, for me to kill my best friend and paint with his blood. My son would still be alive."

"Your friend too." He smiled. "But hindsight is twenty-twenty."

"It is."

"So how is it?" Whoyawanmetabe nodded at the covered picture, disregarding his feelings all together. It was as if he hadn't eaten in weeks and a meal of steak and eggs sat across from him with a succulent aroma. "Is it a work of art?"

Mason looked back at the sheet. "You were right." He paused. "It is my best."

Whoyawanmetabe rubbed his hands together. "Well let me see! Don't make me wait!"

Mason rose and yanked the sheet off revealing the backs of two young friends sitting on the steps in Baltimore city. It was the place Mason and Banks grew up as children. Mason had a low cut and Blakeslee had pigtails running down her back.

It told a sad story.

Of happy times gone by.

Whoyawanmetabe loved it. The richness of the blood colors, which was used to highlight the undertones of Mason's brown skin and the reds of Banks' shirt, were vivid and breathtaking.

Slowly Whoyawanmetabe walked toward the painting, being sure to take in each aspect from afar before moving closer.

Slowly.

Now he could see more details.

The ball on the step next to them. The car flying by and how their heads were tilted slightly so that they were facing each other.

It was utter perfection.

He could *feel* their bond.

Whoyawanmetabe had always been a sucker for the rare, so when he learned about the talented artist from Baltimore who painted his portraits with human blood over twenty years ago, he followed his career.

Had even been to every exhibit.

Of course he was a fan.

He already owned five of his paintings but this one took on new meaning. It was art, created with the blood from the man who stole the love of his early life.

Running his fingers over top of the painting, he smiled as he felt each hardened surface. His fingertips experienced light orgasms retracing Mason's strokes as if they created it together.

The expressions of the young children embedded in the art who had no idea that their lives were going to change called to his soul. He loved the masterpiece so much he ran his nose across the finishing and inhaled deeply.

Pulling back Whoyawanmetabe smiled until...

Suddenly his eyes flapped open and he grabbed his throat. He clawed at his neck with both hands, drawing bloodlines in the process. He couldn't breathe. He couldn't catch air although he desperately tried.

Mason rose slowly when he dropped to the marble floor.

He had waited for this moment and suddenly it didn't seem to matter anymore.

"You have a habit of touching and inhaling things you want to hurt or possess," Mason said.

"I noticed that about you early on. With the way you touched Emetine and even me and Banks on the beach. The painting is rich with poison. And your habit is now the reason you'll die. You can thank Rosa for that part. She's good."

Whoyawanmetabe's skin began to turn a baby blue.

"But you were right about me," Mason continued. "I moved without thinking. Been that way all my life. I should've been patient." He said through tightened teeth. "If only I had been patient, my son...my son..." he choked back tears as Rosa, Ives and Tobias walked inside.

Seeing her work, Rosa took a deep breath as she stared down at Whoyawanmetabe pulling his last breath.

"The cameramen ate our food again last night." She shook her head. "Just as we thought. I guess Banks' plan worked after all. The poison got to them too. He knew what to do."

Mason nodded and looked over at her. "Yeah." He dragged a hand down his face. "He always does."

*It was a warm spring day as Blakeslee tossed a ball back and forth with Mason in front of their building. Maybe it was the atmosphere. Or the cool brisk air. It's been said that the winter brings along a change in those who are willing to accept their fate.*

*But with all certainty, a lot had changed since the last time Blakeslee had spoken to Nikki, starting with the fact that she no longer required her attention. But Blakeslee's physical appearance was also altered. She had traded her two long French braids, for a short cropped curly hairstyle that made her more masculine.*

*Even the way she walked was different. Instead of trying to be like Mason, she adapted an air of confidence and as a result she developed a natural gait that worked for her physique.*

*A bop that was all her own.*

*In the end, she was finally falling into who she really was.*

*Banks Wales.*

*Sure she wanted to be with Nikki. But over the weeks it hurt less. Primarily because since she lost her, she didn't have to go through the pain of losing her again.*

*Blakeslee was moving on with life.*

*Mason was just about to order some pizza, her favorite, when he remembered something he overheard at school.* "Oh, I forgot to tell you, Nikki broke up with Hector."

*Blakeslee shrugged allowing the info to roll off her shoulders like beaded water drops.* "I don't go to that school no more. So you don't have to keep me posted."

*Mason smiled for more than one reason. He had plans to transfer to her new school too but hadn't told her yet.* "So you gonna act like you don't care?"

"I don't." *She widened her grip for the ball.*

*Mason tossed it at her.* "Well if you want, I thought of another plan to get her back. We could—"

"Nah, I'm done playing games, Mason. I'm done chasing her too." *She tossed the ball back.* "Just...just let it go. I have."

*Mason smiled but quickly let his expression disappear like fine mist to cool air. The last thing he*

280                    By T. STYLES

wanted was to appear too happy about her not being with Nikki. "So that mean, you don't, don't wanna be with her no more? You—"

"It means if she don't want me, I gotta be good with it. I mean, I, I don't know how to be nothing more than what I am. So, so, like I said I'm done chasing her. Especially if she think I'm not good enough."

Suddenly, Mason looked past her and his eyes widened. Nikki was coming home.

"What's wrong with you?" Blakeslee asked, seeing the expression change on his face.

"Glad you feel that way because there she go right there." He pointed over her shoulder and she followed his gaze.

At that moment, Nikki was walking toward their building, rubbing her coat covered arms briskly.

The moment she laid eyes on her, Blakeslee could tell she'd been crying. Instead of going inside their building she stopped in front of her. "Blakeslee..." She sniffled. "Can I...can I talk to you for a second?"

"Banks." She stuffed her hands into her pocket. "I go by Banks Wales now. My pops and moms been gave me the name but...I'm...I'm using it *now." She looked back at Mason. "I want you to start calling me that too."*

*Mason nodded and walked away with the ball, leaving them alone.*

*Nikki took a deep breath and wiped the tears away. "I heard you...I heard you changed schools."*

*Banks shrugged. What business was it of hers?*

*"I broke up with Hector."*

*Banks nodded.*

*Nikki stepped closer feeling as if she was sinking in quicksand and losing Banks forever. Why wasn't she excited upon hearing the news? "I'm not getting back with him no more though." She grabbed one of her hands. "We done."*

*Silence.*

*"Blakes...I mean, Banks, do you like me still?"*

*"What difference do it make?" She walked away to be free from her pretty face and leaned against the fence. But Nikki followed, feeling her world slip away. "Even if...even if you are broken up with him, what that got to do with me?"*

*Her eyes widened. "I was saying it because—"*

*"I'm done trying to, trying to make a person like me." She stood up straight. "I mean, I don't know why I am the way I am, but this is it, Nikki. I'm not*

changing." She threw her hands up in the air. "If you can't get with that, step the fuck out my life."

Nikki was stunned into submission. "I don't mind you being like...like you are but—"

"It ain't nothing to mind though. This me. Period. If you like me, you gotta like me like this. What's it gonna be? 'Cause either way I'm good over here. Not chasing you no more. Not letting you hurt my feelings no more either."

Nikki looked around, at the passing cars, at the building's door and finally into Banks' eyes. "I like you, Banks. Always have. And if you give me another chance I'm not fucking up this time. For nobody."

Banks moved closer. "If you gonna be with me, you gotta tell him." Her confidence was on the highest level.

"Hector?"

"Yeah, and to his face. I wanna see it."

"It's done."

Later that day she planned to do just that however Hector and his father were killed in a car accident. Nikki was broken up due to how his death happened but Banks allowed her the time she needed to grieve. Without jealousy. Besides, *there was no need. She understood they were a couple at one point so Banks' only objective was to be there for her girlfriend.*

*And that's what she did.*

*The next day, Banks and Mason were sitting on the stoop eating candy alone. As usual, Mason had enough money to feed the needy. But as they sat and ate the treats, Mason was curious about something. "You different."*

*Banks shrugged.*

*Mason laughed. "I say you different and you brush me off?"*

*Banks looked at him. "What you want me to say?"*

*"I want you to tell me why."*

*Banks sat the candy box down and brushed her hands to remove any crumbs. "Remember Mr. James? Who use to live downstairs?"*

*"Yeah, was always yelling and cussing us out when we played in the hallway."*

*Banks laughed. "And it never worked."*

*Mason nodded. "Nah! Fuck that nigga still. I 'on't care if he moved or not."*

*Banks looked down. "But his wife, Mrs. James, when she opened the door, she used to come out and smile when we were in the hallway. Never*

284 By T. STYLES

said nothing mean and just...asked us to keep it down. She was always so calm and I liked that about her."

"I know...but to be honest she used to scare the fuck outta me. First of all she was tall as fuck and—"

"I'm serious!"

"Okay, dang," Mason said.

"Anyway you were scared of her because you didn't know, like, where she was coming from. Because she was always cool."

Mason nodded finally understanding what Banks was saying.

"I'm gonna move like Mrs. James for the rest of my life," Banks continued. "Calm. Because all that other shit don't be working. Not for me anyway." Banks shrugged, picked up the candy box and started eating again.

Minnie, Joey, Shay, Cassandra, Roxana, Derrick, Spacey, Bet, Jersey, Howard and

Patterson sat on the sectional in the living room, looking up at Tobias, Rosa, Ives, and Mason who stood before them. The room was tense but what they also noticed almost immediately was that there were no cameras.

The Lou brothers were happy to see Jersey back because after she exposed her weapon, the cameramen knocked her down and removed it, later taking her in the lockdown room below the house.

But where were Whoyawanmetabe and his men now?

"I want to say something," Mason said quietly. "Before we go any further I want to say that I wasn't...I didn't know about any of this until the last minute."

Everyone frowned, as their eyes looked to one another for some clue of what he was referring to. They were already on edge after dealing with Banks' death. Their hearts couldn't take much more.

"Pops, what's this all about?" Patterson asked moving uneasily in his seat. "Just say it."

Mason was about to speak until Rosa interrupted and said, "Please remain calm first. And then we'll tell you." Her voice was low but her words were firm. When everyone settled down she turned her head, looked at the doorway and took a deep breath. "Mr. Wales."

The room was thick with gasps.

Who was she calling?

Everyone sitting on the sofa widened their eyes except Jersey, as Banks walked into the room limping but alive. Although shot in the upper body, the blow impacted his gait. As far as they knew he was buried days earlier and that was the end of it but they were wrong.

What was that thing that they buried?

Packed and shaped wet sheets?

Not aware, Bet fell dizzy and almost hit the floor from a seated position. Had it not been for her sons, she would've landed face first on the marble.

Minnie on the other hand ran up to Banks and hugged him tightly. All of the pain, all of the hate she felt for her mother prior was released and turned into love for Banks. She didn't care why he was alive, just that she was able to hold him again. And although he was in pain due to the bullet wound, he welcomed the embrace.

In awe, the others quietly talked among themselves, afraid that they were dreaming.

"Sit down, sweetheart," Banks said softly. "I have a lot to explain."

Minnie held him tighter and slowly she returned to her seat, happily clutching Shay's hand.

"Dad...what...what's going on?" Spacey asked mouth hung open. Body trembling.

"After Jersey told us who Whoyawanmetabe really was, I realized what he wanted. Every painting Mason had done out of blood was *personal*." Banks swallowed the lump in his throat. "So I knew he wanted this one to be personal too. And what better way to do that then by killing me and using my blood? It was the reason the other painting he created of himself didn't work. He didn't even use Arlyndo's blood."

"Pops, you said you knew about this later." Patterson said. "Did ma know too?"

"I was a part of the original plan," Jersey admitted speaking for her husband. "We only told your father after the fact. So when he was painting he thought Banks was dead." She rose and stood next to Banks. "We figured it would be more real if Mason didn't know because—"

"They didn't tell me 'cause they thought...they knew I'd probably fuck it up," Mason said. "Like I, like I did with Arlyndo."

Everyone silently agreed.

"But the blood...there was so much of it," Minnie said. "I saw your body, dad."

"You didn't see my body. They shaped sheets heavy with water. And the Nunez family and Jersey had been draining their own blood for days," Banks moved closer. "I had a clinic built in their home for first aid care a while back. For blood transfusions, cuts, broken bones and stuff like that since we aren't near a hospital. Rosa spent time as a nurse in the war in her country, and had some knowledge on blood draws and how to heal some illnesses. It was another reason I hired her family."

Everyone was stunned at Banks' level of preparation.

"But we had to be safe." He continued. "The amount of blood we needed could've killed someone." He sighed. "That's why they'd been drinking tons of water. That's why they've also been weak and eating fruit and sweet treats. To control their blood sugar because we had to collect enough to convince Whoyawanmetabe that I'd actually died. I thought of every inch of this plan. Even knowing that the last time I planned something like this, Harris died and I could've died too." He looked down. "But I had to take a chance."

"So..." Both Derrick and Shay spoke at the same time.

He smiled at her. "You can...you can go first."

Shay nodded, took a weighing breath and looked at Banks. "So, the thing with uncle Mason and Bet was planned too?"

Banks glared but then released the tension in his face. It didn't matter because everyone had seen the expression that he couldn't take back. And so they had their answer.

"The plan was to get Mason mad at me and Jersey over us getting closer. That way she would pull the gun and fake shoot him but I would jump in the way. No one knew that Bet and Mason would sleep with each other but we used that incident to our advantage. The code to alert Tobias that we were moving on the plan was by yelling, *'I'M SICK OF EVERYTHING AND EVERYBODY IN THIS MANSION!'* Which Jersey did, so the Nunez family came running to execute their part. Everything was thought out." He looked at his wife and Mason. "But their affair."

"So mom did fuck uncle Mason," Minnie snapped.

"Minnie, not right here...not like this," Banks said.

Minnie calmed down.

"But you were actually shot," Derrick said, trying to divert the attention from his father's whorish ways.

"He was," Tobias said. "By me." He stepped up. "I shot him from across the room. The gun Jersey had was blank. We didn't want him to get hit that close. And we knew the commotion would throw everyone else off from which direction the shot rang out."

"But I thought they took all the weapons." Patterson said.

"They did, but—"

"We had a few hidden," Tobias explained, interrupting Jersey. "He didn't know about those. They were in my sister Emetine and Arlyndo's graves. We snuck them out, fearing Whoyawanmetabe would find them. When it was time to use them, we dug the weapons up. And had to rebury their bodies due to desecrating their graves."

Minnie took a deep breath. "So Whoyawanmetabe is dead?"

"Yes. The cameramen too," Banks added.

"But I thought we couldn't kill him because we didn't know who he really was," Minnie continued.

"But we *do* know him don't we?" Banks said looking at Bet. "While I was trying to get more information on him in private, I thought about what your mother said to me when we were in the room one night."

Her sons, who had been holding her hand, released her as all eyes fell on their mother.

"She said, *'He always starts shit when he doesn't get what he wants.'* And I thought, how could she know what he *always* wants unless she knew him? But when? She never dealt with him back in the states. That was all me. With some time, I was able to get a hold of a secret phone in the Nunez house and found out they used to date from her mother. I know longer was concerned about his reach or him being in business with Nidia. His beef was between me, Bet and Mason."

"The bodies, where are they?" Joey asked. "Of the cameramen? And the pilot."

Banks looked at Rosa. "A friend of the Nunez's had them all removed. Buried on this island. Including the pilot." Murdering the pilot made Banks angry but he understood why he had to go. He was essentially a witness. "But let me worry about all of that. For now, I'm gonna fly you all home."

"But you're still hurt," Minnie said.

"I have my co-pilot," Banks said winking at Spacey. "So we good."

Banks sat in his lounge looking for a drink in his bar when Mason strolled inside. Feeling his presence, he looked back at him and shook his head. "So it's true. You really did drink up all my shit. I thought I had enough stashed for a year at least." Banks flopped on the sofa. He moaned when the bullet wound stung a little.

"Can we talk?" Mason asked, tucking his hands in his pocket.

Banks looked up at him, his face still battered and bruised. Quite frankly it looked as if he'd been through hell.

But by now Mason knew it was Banks' plan to get him to fight him so hard. He needed it to look real.

"About what, Mason?"

"The thing with Bet, I'm...I'm sorry." He ran a hand down his face. "I didn't know things were going to go that far. I didn't know...we would...I mean."

Banks smiled and shook his head softly. "Are you sorry? I mean are you really? Or are you sorry you got caught? Because there's a difference, man."

"I'm sorry for it all." He sat on the sofa but Banks scooted away. "This, this shit been ripping me up inside. I mean...when I lost my son."

"Don't do that!" Banks pointed at him. "Don't put Arlyndo in it. I lost my son too but I didn't fuck Jersey behind your back."

"It's different! He was my blood."

Banks' eyes widened. "Wow." He fell back in the sofa.

"I didn't mean it that way! I...I..." Mason felt as if he was making matters worse. "Of course he's your son."

Silence.

"You were my best friend, even through the fire," Banks said softly. "And you destroyed that." He rose.

Mason flopped back. "So is there anything...anything I can do at all? Say the word and it's done."

"You can do something."

"You got it," he repeated.

"For once, stay out my life." Banks walked out leaving him alone.

# CHAPTER TWENTY-FOUR

The plane was in flight.

Banks and Spacey spoke quietly about the weather conditions and how to avoid the pending storm headed their way. If he chose to go through the meaty clouds, turbulence would be bad for all aboard but they'd get there sooner. If he chose to go above the clouds, he would add about thirty minutes to a smoother flight, something he wasn't interested in doing, considering everyone aboard still looked at him as if he were a ghost.

He was preparing to make a decision when Bet approached him, rubbing her elbows repeatedly as if cold. "Banks, can we...can we talk?"

He sighed deeply.

"I have the controls, Pops," Spacey said. "Talk to ma."

Banks nodded and walked over to the side where a loveseat sat in the cockpit. They both sat down. "What is it?" He fell back into the sofa, rubbing his knees twice.

"I thought about the poisons that Rosa made and I'm not sure, but I believe Oswalda was

By T. STYLES

poisoning me. Before you returned to the island. When the three of us were alone."

Banks didn't doubt it but he knew she was making an excuse for her weird behavior. The thing was, she'd been crazy in Maryland. "Could be."

"Is it true that you...you gave the Nunez family the house?" She placed a strand of hair behind her ear. "Because if it's true what she did to me, she doesn't deserve anything."

"It was their house to begin with." He crossed his arms over his chest. "Well, the land anyway. I don't want to get into much more right now."

"Can you, I mean, I know you don't want to talk to me." She looked down. "Since what happened, happened to you—"

"When Whoyawanmetabe first came on the property and he avoided the Nunez house, it made sense. They weren't there. But when they returned, and he killed Emetine, I wondered why he kept the cameras away from their home still."

"So, so why?"

"Because he found out later who they really were." He paused. "And he was afraid."

"Delray has never been afraid of anything in his life."

He smirked. Since the truth was out that she knew him, she sat too comfortably in this space. Technically he felt well within his rights to steal her in the jaw for the deceit but it wasn't worth it, not anymore.

"I'm sorry," she said touching his leg. "For saying his name like that."

He glared.

She removed her hand.

"Like I said, he *was* scared." Banks repeated. "He knew that he fucked with the wrong family. He didn't see them coming. Thought it was just us."

"Did you?"

"No...and now it's too late."

"What does that mean?"

He sighed deeply and looked over at Spacey who was handling the controls with confidence. He looked so comfortable and at peace at the helm that he wondered if the flying bug didn't come for him too. It made him proud that one of his children could possibly follow in his footsteps. But whether he did or didn't, Banks would not force him.

298          By T. STYLES

"We going through the storm," Banks said to Spacey having made a decision. He looked back at her. "And I'm done with you."

"Banks, can we—"

She was speaking to herself, because he had already taken his position back with Spacey where he belonged.

## SIX MONTHS LATER

The sky was gray because a winter storm was coming.

Banks sat comfortably in the luxurious study inside his mansion in Maryland looking at the box of memory cards and cameras Whoyawanmetabe used to record the families. At one point he wanted to look at them, but now couldn't bring himself to see the footage.

When his housekeeper walked inside he covered the box with the lid. An older black woman with a gray bun and loving spirit, he liked her the moment he laid eyes on her. "Sir, Mason is here."

Banks tossed his pen and dragged his hands down his face. "Let him in, Gemma."

She nodded and walked away.

A few seconds later, Mason entered, a whole ten pounds lighter as if he had the pounds to spare. Dressed in a waist length chocolate fur coat dusted with droplets of melted snow. "I see you cut your hair." He pointed at Banks' short-cropped curly style. "I liked it better long."

"I know. Anything to make me look like a woman." Banks said laughing once. "That was always your thing."

Mason was surprised he mentioned being a *woman* because in the past he avoided such topics like the plague.

"What's wrong with you?" Banks asked.

"Uh, nothing, I guess, it's just that you don't normally talk about being a...you know." He shook his head. "Even got me scared to say the word and I love pussy."

"I do too, nigga." Banks took a long pause. "But you remember Mr. James?"

Mason stared at him crazily. "You playing right? The nigga used to run us out the apartment building when we were too loud in the hallway. But his wife—"

"It wasn't his wife. She was trans."

Mason was shocked. "Nah...how...how you know?"

"I always knew. Just never said a word. Wanted it to stay her secret." He paused. "And outside of the calm way she was all the time, which is how I built my life, I loved how she stood in her power. No matter what they did to her. I mean, they threw wet shit at her windows...her car. Called her faggy and she still knew who she was."

"I threw some shit at her car a couple of times too but it was only because she looked strong in the face." He laughed. "I ain't know she was a man until now."

"I know what you did and it always fucked me up. It was another reason why even though we were close, we were never as close as we could've been, because I would say to myself if he could do that to her, what would he do to me?"

Mason felt bad. This was not how he wanted to show up at his house. "It's different with you."

"Maybe." Banks shrugged. "I ain't know that back then. Anyway, through it all, nothing bothered her. She didn't leave that building until her husband died. Took everyone's jabs and held her head high everyday. Not me though. After losing the island I worked all my life to build I realized that I was running. Away from other niggas who didn't deserve my pain. How could I say I'm like her when I broke her code?" He paused. "Well I'm through with that. And I'm not saying I'm not fucked up when people throw who I am in my face, but what I'm not gonna do is take shit to my heart. No more hiding. Which is another reason I gave up the island." He paused. "The nigga Whoyawanmetabe made me realize it was my personal hell."

Silence.

"So...what do you want?" Banks continued.

"First off, I'm surprised you told her to invite me in this time." Mason continued, looking back at the door. "I've been trying to get you to let me in for, what, five months now?"

"Six, now what do you want?" He motioned for him to sit down on the sofa in front of his desk.

Mason eagerly took position. "I heard Bet moved out," he stuffed his hands into his coat pockets.

"So this is what you choose to talk to me about?" He walked around his desk and sat on the edge. He was now looking down at Mason. "My wife that you fucked behind my back?"

"I'm just—"

"It doesn't even matter." Banks raised his hand. "I already filed for a divorce." Banks paused. "We over. So you, you keeping in touch with her? Ya'll some type of weird couple who—"

"Nah, I don't talk to her," he said waving the air. "That's long done. Howard says she lives in the same building he does though. In them high rises in downtown Baltimore."

"Oh yeah, was surprised to hear that Howard moved out from the nest. Figured he would live with you forever."

"Nah, things, things changed and it was time for him to bounce." Mason paused, remembering how he walked in on him raping Spacey. They hadn't been the same since. To be honest it ripped him up that his own son reminded him of his uncle so he had to break ties. "Listen, man,

I'm here to tell you I'm moving." He readjusted in his seat. "To L.A."

Banks' heart dropped and he shifted uneasily although he didn't know why. Since neither was no longer communicating, he was surprised the news hit him so hard. "So what's in, what's in L.A.?" Banks crossed his arms over his chest.

"Change. Me, Jersey, Patterson and Derrick. All going. Although I think she gonna try and divorce me once we move. She been acting different. But since Jersey hit them cops before we left for the island, it's a possibility that they're going to blame us so she needs me. Right now they can't find the bodies but...I'm sure they'll try to make something stick soon."

Banks nodded in agreement. He had forgotten about the reason the Lou's had to retreat to the island in the first place. "Good move. I hope it works out for you."

"But that's why I'm here. Before I leave, I wanted to make sure you don't need me." He looked up at him. "For...for whatever promise you made to the people who helped back on the island. The ones who got rid of the bodies."

"Mason, I—"

"I'm serious, man. I know you see me as a fuck up. By the way I acted on the island, and even when we were kids, I understand why. But I'm here now. You know? I know we in our forties in this bitch but a nigga still got some growing up to do." His chest heaved with a heavy breath. "I guess what I'm trying to say is...before I go, I wanna make sure that you don't need me. Because on God I'd drop everything for you."

Banks thought about what was facing him in the future. A bigger foe than he ever thought he'd have to deal with in life. Bigger than Nidia even. And he didn't want anybody he loved near the chaos.

Not even his arch nemesis.

"It's my problem."

Mason nodded. "You sure because I can—,"

"Mr. Wales, there are a lot of men outside your home." His maid said looking shook.

Banks rose from the desk. "Did they knock on the door?"

"No, they're just...just looking." She seemed frazzled and was even trembling. "It's very weird."

It was time.

Banks nodded, walked over to the doorway and touched her on the shoulder. She calmed instantly. "Remember I was telling you that working for me could be heavy at times? But you still wanted the job because you needed the money."

She nodded yes. Under his employ she already bought a house and two cars for her girls.

"Well this is the heavy part." He paused. "Go to your room and close the door. Don't come out unless I knock."

When he exited his office his phone buzzed. Removing it from his pocket he saw it was a text from Jersey.

*I miss u already.*
*I don't regret last night.*
*Do you?*
*Please call me.*

"Who that?" Mason asked.

Banks quickly stuffed his phone back into his pocket. "Nobody."

When he made it to the door, he saw Joey, Spacey, Shay and Minnie were already in the foyer, staring outside. But it was Minnie who shocked him because he wasn't certain, but he could've sworn he saw the handle of a gun on her waistline.

And then there was the look on her face.

One that he didn't see before but she appeared regal, strong and powerful. Something like a young Nidia and it shocked him to the core.

Remembering the strangers, he walked past them, with Mason at his side. He didn't bother telling his children to go to their rooms, they'd already been exposed to life.

Winter was here.

The snow was heavy and turned everything with color white. Still, stepping outside, Banks saw a sea of men dressed in fine coats, standing in front of BMW trucks.

In protection mode, the Wales clan moved behind their father.

A Latino man, flanked by two armed men walked toward the house when they saw Banks. One was holding a red umbrella over his head while the protected man had an eerie smile on his face.

"Dad, I saw him on the island," Joey whispered. "When you were gone."

Banks nodded as the Latino man approached. A mechanical grin covered the stranger's face. "My name is Mr. Bolero and I represent the man who helped you and the Nunez family on Skull Island."

Banks frowned, snow falling over his head. "Skull Island?"

He laughed. "Mr. Wales, before you buy property you should know the history. Unfortunately for you, you failed to do the work and now you owe."

"But I gave them the land," Banks said.

"Exactly, so why you here?" Mason added.

Bolero stared with intensity at them both. "Does the land mean to get rid of the point that my boss lost two daughters? Emetine and Oswalda Nunez?"

Now Banks was definitely confused.

"What do you want?"

Mr. Bolero clapped his hands once. "To bring understanding. It is the reason I'm here." He raised his hand, all five fingers pointed to Banks' door. "Shall we began?"

Made in the USA
Monee, IL
17 November 2021